Pizza pete

AND THE PERILOUS POTIONS

GUPPY BOOKS

CARRIE SELLON

Pizza pete

AND THE PERILOUS POTIONS

ILLUSTRATED BY Sarah Horne

GUPPY BOOKS

PIZZA PETE AND THE PERILOUS POTIONS
is a GUPPY BOOK

First published in the UK in 2023 by
Guppy Books,
Bracken Hill,
Cotswold Road,
Oxford OX2 9JG

Text copyright © Carrie Sellon
Inside illustrations © Sarah Horne

978 1 913101 954

1 3 5 7 9 10 8 6 4 2

Papers used by Guppy Books are from well-managed
forests and other responsible sources.

GUPPY PUBLISHING LTD Reg. No. 11565833

A CIP catalogue record for this book is available from the British Library.

Typeset by Falcon Oast Graphic Art Ltd
Printed and bound in Great Britain by CPI Books Ltd

For Immie, Freddie and Tallulah.
I promise never to put pineapple on your
pizza again.

In my last English lesson, Miss Cameron asked us for our favourite word. Eight people said 'football'. Three said 'fart'. One said 'onomatopoeia'.

I didn't put my hand up, but I carefully wrote four letters in my exercise book.

H-O-M-E.

That's my favourite word. The cosiest word in the English language. Home. A place where no one laughs at me for the stuff I'm rubbish at, like football and diving. And I have hours and hours to get on with the stuff I'm good at, like making pizzas and building interplanetary warships out of Lego.

That English lesson was the last time I was at school. It was twenty-five days ago. Something *awful* happened the next day, and I made a promise to myself.

Never to leave home again.

Chapter One

I pushed the last Lego brick into place in my Imperial Star Destroyer and stepped back to admire it. The most awesome spaceship in the entire *Star Wars* universe, completed in approximately nineteen hours, thirty-two minutes and fourteen seconds.

'Oi! Pete!'

My stomach flipped as I looked out of my open bedroom window and saw Archie Boyle. He was in the middle of the road, kicking a football with Zach Manson.

'Where've you been all term?' called Archie, picking up the ball. 'You're not at school. You're not delivering pizzas. What's wrong with you?'

'It's his brain,' said Zach. 'He's eaten so many pizzas his brain's turned to cheese.'

Archie stared up at me, shielding his eyes from the

sun. 'I'm not going till you tell me.'

Heat spread up my neck. Archie was the last person I'd tell. 'Just go away, or I'll . . . I'll . . .'

'You'll what? Attack me with your lightsaber?'

I flung the curtains shut to block out the whoops of laughter, accidentally knocking my Lego shelf. The Star Destroyer wobbled towards the edge. I lunged for it, both hands out. But not fast enough. It smashed into a million pieces – well, four thousand, seven hundred and eighty-four to be precise – clattering onto the wooden floor like hailstones.

'Pete?' Dad shouted up the stairs. 'Are you OK?'

'Yup,' I groaned, digging my knuckles into my eyes to stop myself crying. Part of me wished I'd never won the stupid spaceship in the first place.

'You're on dough balls this morning, remember?' called Dad. 'I'm back in an hour. Love you.'

Pulling on my favourite hoodie, I went downstairs. There was no sign of Archie or Zach outside the shop. They must have gone around the corner onto the high street. My shoulders dropped a couple of inches.

I checked the time – nine o'clock. Two hours till opening time. I loved it when The Little Pizza Place was closed, and I had the shop to myself and all was peaceful and quiet.

A loud crackle came from the huge, domed, brick pizza oven in the corner, behind the service counter. I pulled on Dad's welding gloves and carefully added a few logs to the fire, using the shovel to move them around. The key to making the oven super-hot was to make sure all the wood was burning and the entire oven floor was covered.

Now for the dough balls. In the kitchen, at the back of the house, I measured the flour, yeast and

salt into the giant mixer. Then I stirred in the olive oil and milk, and gradually added the warm water. Flicking the switch, I watched the dough hook going around and around. There's something strangely relaxing about watching dough being kneaded until it changes consistency, becoming smooth and elastic. When it was ready, I divided it into sixteen balls and put them in the proving drawer to puff up.

Dad came back while I was sitting at the service counter eating toast and destroying dragons on my phone. Usually his curly hair was covered in flour and a bandana was tied around his forehead. Today there was no flour and no bandana. He looked like he'd been scrubbed with a washing-up brush.

He peered into the pizza oven then squeezed my shoulder. 'Make your old man a coffee, will you?'

When I came back from the kitchen, he was sitting at the counter staring into the middle distance. He smiled at me as I slid his favourite mug in front of him.

I pulled up a stool. Something wasn't right. Usually when Dad smiled his eyes twinkled and you couldn't help but smile back. This time it was different. Like the light had gone out.

He rubbed the back of his neck. 'I've just been to the bank.'

I squirmed. I never usually asked for anything, but last night I'd asked why my pocket money hadn't gone up on my birthday.

He'd said, 'Money doesn't grow on trees, you know,' which I said was a ridiculous thing to say because *obviously* money doesn't grow on trees. But then I'd felt bad because Dad said the cost of flour had gone through the roof, and *then* the conversation moved onto Fox Pizza, like it always did.

Fox Pizza was the new takeaway place in the shopping centre, run entirely by robots. There were hundreds of Fox Pizzas. Dad had been tracking their growth with pins on a huge map in the kitchen. The first few opened in London, then Manchester, Liverpool, Glasgow. And then they exploded, all over the country. It was only a matter of time before one came to Accringham. It opened to huge fanfare and excitement. Everyone was *obsessed* with it – most of our customers had deserted us. Yesterday, we only sold three pizzas. One to Mr Campbell at number seventy-four and two to Mrs Afolabi on the high street.

Dad slowly stirred his coffee, the spoon clinking on the inside of the mug. 'There's no easy way to say this, but the truth is . . . the truth is we've run out of money, and I've fallen behind with the repayments to the bank.'

I squeezed his hand. He was always worrying about money, and we always managed somehow. 'I could sell some of my Lego?'

He closed his eyes for a second, then looked straight into mine. 'They're going to evict us.'

'Evict?'

'They're throwing us out of our home, love.'

I jumped up, knocking the stool over. 'What? They can't do that! Where are we going to live?'

He put my stool the right way up. 'Craig said we can stay at the pub until we find somewhere. This place is falling apart anyway. It needs someone to come in and smarten it up.' I followed his gaze to the peeling paint next to the pizza oven. When Dad wasn't making pizzas he was fixing taps, patching up walls and filling cracks. I didn't notice the cracks. It was home. I'd never lived anywhere else.

He reached over to take my hand. 'Maybe it'll be good for us. It'll force you to—'

'Don't say it!' I pulled my hand away, anger knotted through my body.

He paused, a tiny muscle flickering in his cheek. 'You can't hide in your room for the rest of your life. You've stopped going to school, despite my best efforts to make you go. You've stopped helping me with deliveries. You've stopped *living*. There's a whole world out there, waiting for you. How are you going to see it if you're hiding in your room playing video games all day?'

9

I crossed my arms. 'I'm not hiding. I *can't* go outside. There's a difference.'

He sighed. 'I'm afraid we've got no choice. The bank's got a possession order to take the house in four days.'

'Four *days*?!'

He looked down, biting his lip. 'They did give us six months, but that was . . . er . . . six months ago.'

'Why didn't you tell me?'

He shrugged. 'I didn't want to worry you.'

'At least I'd have had time to get used to it!'

'Unless—'

'Yes?' I said.

'Unless we can magic up ten thousand pounds.'

'Ten *thousand* pounds?!'

He nodded. 'Ten thousand pounds would get the bank off our backs for another six months. Give us some breathing space.' He took his car keys out of his pocket and went to the door.

I glared at him. 'Where are you going now?'

'Flowerdown. Granny Tortoise had another funny turn this morning.'

I blinked. I missed Granny Tortoise. She used to

live in a tiny cottage with a tortoise called Sid, until she started having funny turns. Then she moved into Flowerdown Care Home. *Flowerdown*. Dad and I thought it was the most depressing name for a care home ever.

He checked his phone then looked up at me. 'She'd love to see you.'

I rolled my eyes – *good try* – and glanced at the clock. 'You'd better be quick. It's only forty-eight minutes till opening time.'

'I might be a bit late, love.'

I frowned. Dad had opened the shop at exactly eleven a.m. and closed at precisely eleven p.m. seven days a week, for as long as I could remember. 'What if we get a customer? I thought we were desperate for money?'

He gave me a weary smile. 'We're never going to make ten thousand pounds in four days.' He came over and ruffled my hair. 'It's going to be OK. We'll always have each other, right?'

As I locked the door behind him, I felt a pressure on my chest, like a long string of mozzarella was wrapping itself around my insides, squeezing tighter and tighter. It was obvious. Dad wasn't even *trying* to come up with the money.

If I wanted to save our home, I'd have to do it myself.

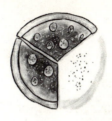

Chapter Two

I was pulling cans of food out of the larder and piling them up on the kitchen table when the doorbell rang.

Anna pushed her glasses up the bridge of her nose and grinned at me through the shop window. She lived opposite, with her mum. We'd been friends ever since my first day in Reception, when I'd squirted ketchup on my face by accident. I'd sat there dying of embarrassment with nothing to wipe it off, until Anna picked up the ketchup and squirted it all over her face too.

When I let her in, her dog, Useless, shot past me and started snuffling around for crumbs. Like her owner, Useless had clearly never heard of a hairbrush – her grey fur was so long and straggly, you could barely tell which end her head was.

I glanced outside to see if any food inspectors

were lurking, then locked the door. 'We'll get in trouble if anyone sees a dog in here. Regulation number—'

'Eight hundred and fifty-two. I know, I know.' Anna clomped into the kitchen in her Doc Martens, her guitar swinging from her shoulder. As usual, she was wearing her purple cardigan and black boilersuit even though it was about thirty degrees out there. 'I had to get out. First day of the summer holidays and already Mum's nagging me about my French project.'

'That's because it was meant to be in before the end of term.' I'd finished mine ages ago. Mr Shah, my form teacher, emailed me every morning with my schoolwork for the day. I didn't mind. There are only so many hours of *Dragon Street* you can play without feeling like your eyes are going to pop out.

Anna opened the larder and reached for the biscuit tin, then plonked herself down at the kitchen table. 'What's all this?' she asked, waving her hand at the piles of food.

We finished off a packet of Jammy Dodgers while I told her what Dad had said, about moving out unless we could come up with ten thousand pounds.

Her eyes widened. 'You can't move! Whose homework would I copy?'

'We're not moving, not if I can help it. I've got an idea.' I went back into the larder, and climbed up on the bottom shelf so I could reach the naughty food at the back. 'Dad's been doing the same old toppings for years. Everyone's bored of mozzarella and pepperoni and olives. We need something new. Something surprising. Something unexpected.'

'Like what?'

I flung a packet of marshmallows onto the table. 'Marshmallow and anchovy?'

'Disgusting!'

'Pringles and beetroot?' I asked.

'Horrible!'

'Peanut butter and tuna?'

'Eww! I'm going to be sick!'

'How do you know until you've tried—'

My phone buzzed. It was a message from Dad.

Granny bit wobbly. I'd better stay. Will open shop when back – 3ish. Love you.

I looked at the clock. 'We've got ages. The dough will be ready soon, then we can play around with new toppings. We have to find something *mind-blowing* to steal our customers back from Fox Pizza.'

Anna's face lit up. 'Have you been there yet?' She put her hands out stiffly in front of her and said in a robotic voice, '*Han-nah, your pi-zza is rea-dy.*'

I glared at her. 'You're not called Hannah.'

'I know, but—'

'They use frozen dough. And their toppings aren't fresh.'

'Listen, your pizzas are way better. It's just that everyone's forgotten about you, stuck down here.'

She was right. The Little Pizza Place was the only shop on Harwood Road. The high street was just at the end of the road, but no one walked past our shop unless they lived down here.

She clapped her hands. 'I know. Let's go up and down the high street with flyers to drum up business. We could dress up as pizzas!'

I scowled at her. 'I *can't*!'

She glanced at my reward chart on the fridge. Dad had pushed all his fridge magnets to the bottom to squeeze it on. I was meant to tick it whenever I left the house. Dad said he'd give me *Dragon Street* 2 when I got five ticks. So far I had a grand total of zero.

Anna's face softened. 'You still haven't been out, have you?'

I shook my head, biting the side of my thumb. Anna was the only person, apart from Dad, who knew the real reason I hadn't been going to school. The *terrible* thing that happened.

It was a Saturday morning, the day after the English lesson when Miss Cameron asked us our favourite word. Dad took me and Anna to Accringham Leisure Centre for my twelfth birthday. They had this obstacle course in the pool which we did a zillion times until my skin was all wrinkly. We were just about to leave when Anna persuaded me to go on the high diving board. All these kids from school were in the queue, shouting at me to jump.

But I couldn't do it. The longer I stood there, the more freaked out I got.

And then, completely out of nowhere, my heart started thumping like crazy, like it was about to explode. I had all this sweat dripping down my face. I didn't know what was happening to me. I thought that was it – the *End*. I was going to die, right there, in my *Star Wars* swimming trunks. Next thing I knew, I was on my hands and knees crawling back along the board. That's when Archie Boyle started shrieking and pointing like it was the funniest thing he'd ever seen.

After the weekend, I refused to go to school. Dad took me to see Dr Shannon. She was really kind and told me I'd had a *panic attack*. She explained what to do if it happened again: sit somewhere calm, slow my breathing, and remember – it would end soon. But the next day, I refused to go to school again. The thought of having another panic attack, at school of all places, was unbearable. I pretended to have a sore head. The day after that, sore ears. Before I knew it, it was the weekend again, and I'd barely left my room. It was my safe place. My cocoon.

That Sunday night, I wiped the steam off the bathroom mirror and made the promise to myself.

Never to leave home again.

Anna was chewing the manky sleeve of her cardigan, watching me. 'Let me get this straight. You've got four days to come up with an ingenious idea to make loads of money, without even stepping out the door?'

'Yup.'

She adjusted her glasses. 'You need a gimlick, like Fox Pizza.'

'I think you mean a gimmick.'

'Yeah, one of those. What could you do? Come on, you're the king of crazy ideas.'

I thought for a moment. 'Pizza boxes that say your name when you open them?'

'Impossible.'

I rubbed my chin. 'Cricket pizzas?'

'Ewww!'

I shrugged. 'We'll all be eating insects in the future. Gobbling up crickets and mealworms for breakfast.'

'I'm going to pretend I didn't hear that.'

'OK. How about flying pizzas?' I said.

'What?'

'We attach the pizzas to a drone and they fly through the air to people's houses. There's a pizza shop in New Zealand doing it.' I googled it on my phone and showed her. 'Their sales have gone up eighty-four per cent.'

Anna smiled. 'You'll do anything to avoid going outside, won't you?'

My cheeks reddened. 'We could launch the drone from the attic. There's a window up there.'

She mulled it over. 'I'd buy a flying pizza. Let's go up and have a look.'

We put the food back in the larder, then went

upstairs. On the landing in between my bedroom, Dad's bedroom and the bathroom, I reached up to pull a hook in the ceiling and the staircase unfolded. I clambered up first, followed by Anna and Useless. I hadn't been up to the attic for years. It was hot, cramped and dusty, filled with suitcases and bulging cardboard boxes. Everything was covered in cobwebs. The only light came from a filthy window overlooking the street.

'We'll have to move some of this stuff to get to the window.' I started stacking boxes on top of each other. 'Are you going to help me? Anna?'

She closed the lid of an enormous trunk and grinned at me. She was wearing a baseball cap with *I Love Spain* written in sequins, and a huge tasselled scarf around her neck. Useless was sitting next to her wearing a snorkel mask.

'What do you think?' she asked, striking a pose.

Anna loved dressing up, singing and acting, all that stuff. She persuaded me to join Drama Club soon after we met. In the first lesson, we had to do an action that reflected our personality. I pretended I was duelling with a lightsaber. Everyone else

did a TikTok dance. I switched to Chess Club the following week.

I glared at her. 'Take it off. It's Mum's.' It made me feel weird, seeing her in Mum's stuff. I don't know why. It wasn't like I remembered her – she died on my second birthday. It had just been me and Dad ever since. Not easy, as he liked to remind me, having to potty train me for nursery while running a pizza shop.

Sometimes I wished Mum were still alive. I'd never told Dad but part of the reason I loved being at home so much was because it made me feel close to Mum. After all, this is where she'd lived. There were memories of her all over the place – in the photos on the stairs, in the stories Dad told about her, even up here, in the attic. If we moved out, I worried we'd completely forget about her.

Anna blinked. 'Sorry.'

She carefully folded the scarf and put it in the trunk, then lay the baseball cap and snorkel mask gently on top of it. Together, we pushed the trunk under the eaves. Useless sniffed the floor where the trunk had been, then frantically scratched the floorboards.

'What's under there?' I got down on my knees. One of the floorboards wasn't nailed down properly, so I pushed on one end and the other end tipped up. Anna caught it and lifted it to the side.

Useless went mental, scrabbling with her paws and getting her nose right down into the space between the floorboards. Like she'd found something. I pushed her out of the way.

There, tucked under the floorboards, covered in cobwebs, was a briefcase.

Chapter Three

It was made of brown leather – hard and sturdy with scuffed corners.

'Treasure!' Anna knelt beside me and wiped the cobwebs off the briefcase. 'Can I get half?'

'Don't be silly. You don't find treasure in real life. Not in Accringham, anyway.'

I unfastened the two metal clasps. The briefcase split in half easily, like a clam. It was full of small identical brown glass bottles, each with a black dropper cap, neatly arranged in rows. They were labelled with curly, old-fashioned handwriting in jet-black ink. I counted them – fifteen in total.

Anna ran her fingers over the labels. 'What are they? Medicine?'

'They look a bit like eye drops.' I took out a bottle labelled *Grow*, unscrewed the cap, and squeezed the dropper to suck up the liquid. It looked like olive oil. I sniffed it – it smelt very faintly of fish-tank water. 'How did Useless smell *that*?'

Anna reached for the dropper cap. 'Dogs can smell a zillion times better than us. Scientific fact.' She held the cap up to her nose. 'Can't you, Useless?' Useless wagged her tail and jumped up, knocking Anna's hand. The cap fell to the floorboards.

'Careful!' I said. Anna screwed the cap back on, while I picked out another bottle, labelled *Wish*. Underneath it said DO NOT USE in big black letters. 'What sort of medicine *is* this?'

We started reading all the labels. As well as *Grow* and *Wish*, there was *Invisibility, Animal, Turbo, Laughter, Agility, Shrink, Glow, Shapeshifter, Voice, Replication, Strength, Intelligence* and *Flight*.

'Hold on. What's this?' Anna pulled out a snippet of newspaper which had been tucked behind the bottles. At the top was a black-and-white photo of a woman with slicked back hair and a long face like a horse.

I took the article from Anna and read the headline out loud, 'SCANDAL AT FIRDALE PHARMACEUTICALS! MAVERICK SCIENTIST SACKED!'

Anna got her phone out. 'Maverick . . . a person who refuses to follow the rules. I like her already.' She looked up. 'Go on then, what did she do?'

I continued to read. 'Top brainbox Professor Silva Tregoning has been FIRED from Firdale Pharmaceuticals for testing medicines on herself.'

'When was this?'

'Dunno. Oh hold on, there's a date at the top: 21st *March 2008.* I think that's the year Mum and Dad bought this place.' I continued reading out loud:

anjay Citra, head boffin at Firdale Pharmaceuticals, revealed all last week. He said, 'People heard strange noises coming from Tregoning's lab – roars, squawks and even the odd moo.'

Apparently Tregoning (42) was self-experimenting – she was using herself as a GUINEA-PIG for the medicines she was testing.

Citra said, 'I sacked her as soon as I found out. We can't have bad apples ruining Firdale's reputation.' The scandal has sent SHOCK WAVES through the pharmaceutical industry.

Anna peered at the bottles in the briefcase. 'Do you think these are the medicines she was using?'

'Maybe. But it doesn't explain what they're doing in our attic.' I looked at the photo of Professor Tregoning again. She had the faintest smile on her lips, but her eyes gave nothing away. What secrets was she hiding? I was about to get out my phone to see if I could find out more about her, when I heard the doorbell, followed by a familiar booming voice.

'Hello? Is anyone there?'

'It's Winterbotters!' I said. 'What's she doing here?' Mrs Winterbottom, as she preferred to be known, was our headmistress. I'd never seen her outside of school.

'Ignore her,' said Anna.

The doorbell rang again.

I checked the time. It was nearly twelve o'clock. Dad wasn't due back for three hours.

'I'll tell her we're closed. Don't move.' I climbed down both sets of stairs and opened the door. 'Good morning, Mrs Winterbottom.'

Not for the first time, it crossed my mind that her big red face was a bit like a pizza, and her hard, dark eyes were a bit like olives (the nasty, bitter ones). She looked me up and down with pursed lips, as if I were an old sardine she'd found at the back of the fridge.

'You don't *look* ill, Peter.'

'Um . . . well . . .'

'You'd better pull yourself together next term, yes? You're missing out on all sorts. Now, where's your father?'

Without waiting for an answer, she strode in as though she were about to take assembly. Useless bounded down the stairs, tail wagging. As soon as she saw Mrs Winterbottom, her ears dropped and her tail flattened between her legs.

Mrs Winterbottom's nostrils flared. 'What is that revolting, smelly creature doing in a pizzeria?'

'She's not a revolting, smelly creature,' said Anna, stomping down the stairs. 'She's Useless.'

'That's patently obvious,' smirked Mrs Winterbottom as Anna took her out to the garden. 'Where's your father, Peter? I'd like to order some pizzas, yes?'

'Pizzas?'

She stepped back to look at the menu over the counter, her right eyebrow halfway up her wrinkly forehead. 'You do sell pizzas, don't you?'

'We do, but—'

'In that case I would like eighteen,' she said.

'Eighteen?'

She squeezed the bridge of her nose. 'Are you going to repeat *everything* I say?'

Anna came back in, giggling. 'Eighteen pizzas? I didn't think you had it in you, Mrs Winterbottom.'

The vein in the middle of Mrs Winterbottom's forehead pulsated. 'If you were more observant, you would have noticed I have company, yes?' She nodded her head towards the window. A coach was parked on the other side of the road. It looked like it was full of teachers – sleeping teachers. It was very strange. I'd

never seen teachers sleeping, but I supposed they had to at some point.

'I took the staff camping for our end of year jolly,' said Mrs Winterbottom. 'We've consumed nothing but rice and beans for twenty-four hours.'

'Hope the windows are open on the coach,' muttered Anna.

If Mrs Winterbottom heard, she chose to ignore it. 'I promised them we'd get pizzas on our way back to school. We couldn't park at Fox Pizza, so here we are.'

Anna elbowed me. 'Charming.'

But all I was thinking was: *typical*. The one time Dad was out. Eighteen pizzas would have been our biggest order in months. I sighed. 'I'm really sorry, but Dad's not here.'

Mrs Winterbottom glanced up. 'So who's upstairs?'

We all looked at the ceiling. There were strange sounds coming from above – little muffled thuds.

'Must be the plumbing,' I said. 'Dad's gone to see Granny. We're closed.'

'Closed?' The vein was about to burst. 'Why didn't you say so in the first place?'

She spun around and strode towards the door but

Anna rushed to block her path. 'We can make pizzas for you. Can't we, Pete?'

I gave her The Look.

Mrs Winterbottom peered at us. 'Aren't you two a bit young to be making pizzas?'

'Oh no,' said Anna. 'Pete's been making them for years. He's the best.'

'In that case—' started Mrs Winterbottom.

'Hold on . . . let me check something.' I dragged Anna to the kitchen. 'You know I'm not allowed to serve customers on my own,' I whispered through gritted teeth.

She gripped my shoulders. 'Think about the *money*. You were the one saying you were desperate to sell more pizzas. Here's your chance.'

I shook my head. 'The dough won't be ready yet.' I opened the proving drawer to show her, but the dough balls had already puffed up into little squishy pillows.

'They look ready to me,' said Anna.

'There are only sixteen. We need eighteen.'

'We'll break some off to make two more. Easy peasy.'

I was torn. I could tell the dough was the best I'd

ever made – light as a feather, almost as soft as Dad's. I took a deep breath. 'OK. But you have to help me tidy up afterwards. You know what Dad's like about mess.'

Anna's eyes sparkled. 'He'll never even know we were here.'

We went back into the shop. 'Have you had a look at the menu?' I said. 'We can do Margherita, Meat Feast, Hawaiian—'

'Or you could try one of Pete's specials,' said Anna. 'Marshmallow and anchovy?'

Mrs Winterbottom frowned. 'We'll have margheritas. Hopefully even you two won't be able to mess up a simple cheese and tomato pizza.'

'What size would you like?' I asked.

'You must be starving,' said Anna. 'Go for large.'

'One is never starving. One is merely peckish.' As Mrs Winterbottom spoke, an enormous rumble erupted from her stomach. She went bright red and coughed, smoothing her hand over the offending area.

Anna raised an eyebrow. '*Very* peckish?'

'Fine,' said Mrs Winterbottom, opening the door.

'Eighteen large margheritas. Bring them out when they're ready, yes?'

'It's going to be about twenty minutes,' I said, glancing at the clock.

'So what are you waiting for?'

'Um . . .' I scratched the back of my head. 'Payment?'

She glared at us. 'I'm not paying until we've eaten. Now hurry up!'

Chapter Four

In the kitchen, I shaped the dough balls like Dad had taught me, tossing and stretching each one to make the base as thin as possible. I wished he were by my side, whistling as he worked. Although I couldn't actually remember the last time I'd heard him whistling.

Anna peered over my shoulder. 'Can't you make them a bit bigger? They asked for *large* pizzas.'

I nudged her out of the way. 'You forced them to have large pizzas.'

'To make *you* more money,' she huffed, nudging me back. 'I won't bother next time.'

I looked down at the pizzas. They *were* a bit on the small side. I couldn't stretch them as much as Dad could, because my hands were half the size of his. What if Mrs Winterbottom refused to pay us?

Pitter! Patter!

I looked up at the ceiling. The noise was getting louder and clearer.

'Do you think it's mice?' asked Anna, dolloping tomato sauce onto each pizza base.

'I'll take a look.' I wiped my floury hands on my apron and went upstairs.

Pitter! Patter!

'It's in the attic,' I shouted. 'I'm going up.' I climbed the stairs and poked my head into the attic space. 'Hold on—' I fumbled for my phone in my pocket, switched on the torch, and swung it around.

My blood ran cold.

Hundreds of silky, translucent lines criss-crossed from one side of the attic to the other. Some of them were attached to beams, others to boxes. I put out a hand to touch one of the lines. It was sticky.

Why did we have a *giant spider web* in our attic?

That explained the noise. To create something that big – 3.85 metres across in my estimation – the spider had to be *massive*. My heart quickened as I pointed the torch into the eaves, but I couldn't see anything apart from old boxes and trunks. I was about to turn off the torch when I spotted the mysterious briefcase.

It was open, where we'd left it.

I ran back down to the kitchen. 'Anna! Remember that bottle cap you dropped? It said *Grow* on it, didn't it? Did any of the liquid spill out?'

'I don't—'

'Follow me!' I put a finger to my lips as we crept back upstairs, and gestured for Anna to squeeze up next to me on the attic steps. When I turned on the torch, Anna nearly lost her footing but I grabbed her just in time.

She stared at the web. 'Is this some kind of joke?'

'It's because of that Grow stuff. You must have spilt it.'

She snorted. 'And a teeny tiny spider licked it up and grew ginormous, then made this . . . this . . . thing.'

'Exactly. Hold this.' I handed my phone to her and clambered through the strands of silk.

'What are you doing?'

I ducked to avoid a silky thread and picked up the briefcase. My heart was thudding with excitement. 'If it did that to a spider, just think what it could do to our mini pizzas!'

Anna shook her head and climbed down the steps.

'Call me when your brain grows back.'

'How else do you explain a web this size? Hold on, I need the torch—'

BEEP! BEEP! A loud horn blared outside.

'That must be Winterbotters. Anna, come back!' In the darkness, I couldn't see the web. I quickly trampled my way through it, hoping the spider wouldn't come after me. Stumbling down the steps, I slammed the hatch closed and took a deep breath.

Opening the briefcase on the kitchen table, I scanned the bottles until I found the one labelled *Grow*. I waved it in Anna's face. 'If there's the tiniest chance this can turn our small pizzas into large ones, then we've got to take it. Otherwise Mrs Winterbottom might not pay us and all this will be for nothing.' I dripped the Grow liquid all over the pizzas.

'This is ridiculous,' said Anna. 'For a start, they'll see it.'

'No they won't. Not if we add lots of mozzarella. That should hide the taste too.'

Anna sighed and started strumming her guitar while I added the mozzarella and oregano to the pizzas, willing them to grow.

Two minutes passed.

Nothing.

BEEP! BEEP!

I poked my head out of the kitchen so I could see the coach. Mrs Winterbottom was leaning on the horn.

'Coming!' I shouted. Using the peel, I slid the pizzas into the oven in batches, then I pulled up a stool and watched them, the heat burning my face. After a couple of minutes, the pizzas had turned golden, but they weren't any bigger. I wiped my forehead with my sleeve. 'It's not working.'

Anna rolled her eyes. 'Of course it's not working.' My face must have dropped because she put her guitar down. 'Don't worry, they look amazing. Hopefully Winterbotters won't mind if they're a bit small.'

I blinked. They *did* look amazing – just as good as Dad's – and the smell of baked dough and melted cheese enveloped me like a warm hug. My tummy rumbled but there was no time to eat now – the pizzas were bubbling. I took them out of the oven while Anna sliced them and put them into boxes.

As I was rushing to get the last pizza out of the

oven, it slid off the peel onto the floor. In a flash, Useless was under my feet, ready to wolf it down, but she gave a funny yelp as soon as she licked it and ran around in circles.

'Useless!' I shouted. 'What are you doing in here?'

'She was whining so I let her in.' Anna knelt to look at her. 'Poor Useless, you enormous bag of idiot. Did you burn your tongue?'

'Poor Useless?' I scooped the pizza off the floor and put it on the counter. 'She licked it! We can't serve a pizza that's been slobbered on by a dog.'

Anna stood up to inspect it. 'Why not?'

'It's got dog hairs all over it for a start.'

She picked off a couple of greasy hairs and wiped them on her cardigan. 'There.'

I puffed out my cheeks. Dad would kill me if he ever found out. He was obsessed with hygiene. 'OK. But put Useless back in the garden – she's caused enough trouble. And hurry up. You're taking the pizzas to the coach.'

'Me? Why can't you do it?'

My chest tightened. 'You know I can't.'

'Come on, Pete. You'd get a tick on your reward chart.'

I shook my head. My hands were clammy, even at the thought of going outside.

'It's literally ten metres away. Go on, you could do with some oxygen.' Anna peered at me. 'You're looking a bit grey.'

I crossed my arms. 'It was *your* idea to serve Winterbotters. You're taking the pizzas out.'

'I *could* take them out, but that's not going to help you, is it? At some point you've got to face the outside world. This is as good a time as any.' Before I had time to think of a comeback, she'd taken Useless out to the garden.

Grumbling to myself, I piled up the boxes. I knew deep down that she was right, which made it even more annoying. I ran upstairs to get Luke Skywalker and Han Solo from my bedside table and put them in my pocket. They were my good luck charms – small, plastic *Star Wars* figures that Dad had given me for my sixth birthday. But the force wasn't with me today. My head was pounding, my hands were trembling and it felt like a family of snakes was writhing around in my stomach.

I picked up half the pizza boxes – I'd have to come

back for the rest. As soon as I kicked open the door, I froze. There was too much air, but I couldn't breathe. Too much space, but my feet were glued to the spot. It was like my body had been taken over by Jabba the Hutt. What if I had another panic attack?

It was right then, with me standing in the doorway like a fat chunk of pineapple, that Archie Boyle appeared.

Chapter Five

Archie made me step backwards as he came into the shop. He grabbed a pizza box off the top of the pile in my arms.

'Put it back! They're for the teachers.' I nodded my head towards the coach.

Archie looked outside, then back at me, his eyes wide with mock horror. 'Is this why you get such good grades? You're bribing the teachers with free pizza?'

'No! They're paying for them,' I said. 'At least, I hope they are.'

He opened the box and took a massive sniff. 'Rank. Everyone knows your dad sells the rankest pizzas in town.' He shoved the box back on top of the pile, almost making me lose my balance.

My blood boiled. I could cope with Archie being horrible to me, but insulting my dad made me *really* cross. How dare he? And it wasn't true. Dad's pizzas were the best in the world.

'Well . . . well . . . everyone knows *your* dad sells the rankest cars in town,' I said.

A flicker of something passed across Archie's face. He stepped back and I thought he was going to hit me, but he just hissed, 'It's caravans, idiot.' He tried to slam the door on his way out, but it was a slow-closing door, which made him even crosser, so he swore at me before stomping off.

BEEP! BEEP! BEEP! BEEP!

'I'm coming. I'm *coming!*' I shouted, furious that I had to psych myself up for going outside again. I sent all my anger down to my legs and kicked the door open, just as Anna ran back in from the garden.

'What are you still doing here?' she asked.

'I was about to go but—'

'They're getting cold. Hand them over.'

I gave her the pizzas, rubbed my aching wrists and let her out.

'Can you take a look at Useless?' she shouted over her shoulder. 'Her ear's gone a bit weird.'

Useless was sitting on the doormat outside the

back door. One of her ears *did* look a bit odd, although it was hard to see anything with all that fur going on. She started whimpering when I closed the door, so I let her in and she curled up under the kitchen table.

Once Anna had gone back out with the second lot of pizzas, I filled the sink with bubbles and did the washing up, humming the *Star Wars* theme tune to myself. I couldn't wait to tell Dad how much we'd made. If Winterbotters paid for eighteen large pizzas – and it was a big *if* – we'd make two hundred and seventy pounds! OK, it wasn't anywhere near ten thousand pounds, but it was the biggest order we'd had in a long time.

'How's Useless?' Anna came into the kitchen and looked under the table as I was drying up. 'Nooooo!'

My heart skipped a beat as I looked down.

One of her ears was huge – almost twice the size of the other one. It reminded me of *my* ear when Archie Boyle punched me for coming first in the Times Tables Rock Stars competition.

The hairs on the back of my neck tingled as I crouched down and touched it. It was as squishy as a marshmallow. I looked at Anna. 'It's that Grow medicine. It *did* work after all. She must have licked some of it off that pizza that fell on the floor.'

Anna frowned. 'It didn't make the pizzas grow.'

'Maybe it only works on living creatures. Like spiders and dogs.'

She took her glasses off and chewed one of the arms. 'Maybe Useless is allergic to pizza. My uncle Jim's got a cockapoo who's allergic to carrots. He gets these enormous—'

'Useless is *not* allergic to pizza. She's always eating your crusts.' I stood up and took the Grow bottle out of the briefcase. 'It's got to be this. And if one lick has done this to *her* . . .' I looked down at Useless who was squirming at my feet, then peered out of the kitchen at the coach, '. . . what on earth is a whole pizza going to do to *them*?'

'Look! Miss Cameron's opened her pizza box,' I said.

We were hiding in the kitchen, peeking out of the door so we could see the teachers, hopefully without them seeing us.

I held my breath as our English teacher picked up her pizza and took a bite. And another. And another.

Within a minute she'd demolished the lot.

'Monsieur Audibert's eating his,' said Anna. 'And Mr Shah.'

Miss Cameron was wiping her mouth with a tissue. I couldn't see her ears but if one of them was growing, surely *she* would have noticed by now.

I let out a huge sigh and threw a cloth at Anna. 'I think we're OK. Help me tidy up. We haven't got long till Dad gets back.'

'What about Useless?'

We looked at her. Her other ear had swelled up

too. It looked like they'd both been pumped up like balloons.

Just then the shop door opened. 'Hello!' called a voice.

'It's Miss Cameron,' I whispered to Anna. 'You go.'

'No, you go!' she whispered back, shoving me out of the kitchen.

Miss Cameron was standing by the counter, a hand covering her mouth. 'Do you have a mirror, Peter?'

'In here,' I said, showing her into the loo under the stairs.

A few seconds later she burst out. 'Help!' she shrieked, flapping her hands.

My stomach lurched.

Her chin was as long as a carrot.

If my eyes could have pinged out of my head, they would have. I rubbed them, convinced I was seeing things, but there Miss Cameron stood, trying and failing to cover her spiky chin with her hands.

'What's happening to me?' wailed Miss Cameron.

Anna coughed. Her face was as white as mozzarella. 'It could be an allergic reaction. My uncle Jim's got this cockapoo—'

'But I'm not allergic to anything!' Miss Cameron rushed into the kitchen, knocking her chin on the doorframe as she spun around. 'Where's your father, Peter? That pizza's the only thing I've eaten for two days.'

'Um . . . he's out. He'll be back soon.' My heart was thumping in my chest as I checked the time: 2.10 p.m. He really *was* going to be back soon, and what on earth was I going to tell him?

Suddenly the door was flung open and Monsieur Audibert burst in.

My whole body started shaking with nerves, as if I'd swallowed an electric eel. Monsieur Audibert's nose, which had always been on the generous side, was as large as a turnip. A blotchy, red turnip with hairy nostrils you could get lost in. His eyes widened when he saw Miss Cameron. 'Vous aussi?'

The door opened again and Miss Farr came in, her lips swelling up like two rubber tyres. 'Blot bloz blin blat beeza?' she demanded.

Anna and I exchanged a look.

'I think she's asking what was in the pizza,' said Miss Cameron.

Miss Farr nodded violently, her huge lips blobbing up and down.

'Um . . . flour,' I stammered, 'and yeast and—'

'What are you waiting for?' Anna opened the door. 'Go and stop the other teachers from eating theirs!'

'Oh yes, we must!' said Miss Cameron. She let out a sob and ran out of the shop, swiftly followed by Monsieur Audibert and Miss Farr.

'That got rid of them.' Anna turned to me. 'What do we do? Pete?'

I was finding it hard to breathe properly. My heart was hammering, as if a flock of birds were trapped in my chest. I stumbled past Anna, up the stairs.

'Where are you going?' she asked.

Slamming my bedroom door, I took a deep breath. The air felt lighter in here, clearer. I glanced at the photo of Mum on the bedside table. *Mum? Any ideas?*

If only she were here. She'd know what to do.

Picking up some of the Lego from my Star Destroyer, I carefully placed it on the duvet. There were a few chunks that hadn't come apart. If I started now, it wouldn't take too long to repair the damage.

Anna burst in as I was attaching a turbo-laser to the ship. Useless followed, her big ears bouncing around like bags of jelly. 'What do you think you're doing?' cried Anna.

I ignored her. There was a real knack with turbo-lasers. You had to get them in at just the right angle.

'You can't hide up here and pretend nothing's happening.' She ran to the window.

I searched under the bed for an ion cannon. Where had it gone? I had to find it. Whoever heard of a Star Destroyer with only one ion cannon?

Anna had her face pressed to the window. 'It doesn't look like anyone else has reacted.' She suddenly pulled the curtains shut and spun around to face me.

'What's wrong?' I said.

'Winterbotters has spotted me – she's about to explode.'

'Literally?'

'Obviously not literally. With anger.'

I got up and lifted the edge of the curtains. I couldn't see Winterbotters. She must have gone to the other side of the coach. I peered down the street. If anyone was filming this, it would be all over the internet in a flash. *SHOCKING PIZZA SCANDAL – SCHOOLKIDS TURN THEIR TEACHERS INTO MUTANTS!*

Anna grabbed my arm. 'We've got to call your dad.'

'No way!'

'So what do we do? Call an ambulance?'

I paced up and down. 'What do we tell them?'

'The truth. We found freaky potions in the attic. And you're a total idiot and splashed one of them all over our teachers' pizzas.'

I stared at her. 'What did you say?'

'You're a total idiot.'

'No, the other bit.'

'We found freaky potions in the attic?'

'You're a genius!' I raced down to the kitchen, followed by Anna and Useless.

'What are you doing?'

Opening the briefcase, I scanned the labels until I found what I was looking for. 'They're *potions*, not medicine.'

Anna blinked. 'I was joking. This isn't a fairy tale. You don't get *potions* in real life.'

'Whatever you want to call them . . . The stuff in the Grow bottle made everything bigger.' I picked out the bottle labelled *Shrink*. 'I reckon this one will make everything smaller.'

Anna raised an eyebrow. 'You reckon?'

'Got any better ideas?'

She shook her head.

I took a slice of ham out of the fridge, unscrewed the cap on the Shrink bottle and measured a couple of drops onto the ham. Anna knelt down and offered it to Useless. Her tongue shot out and the ham disappeared in one gulp. For a few seconds, nothing happened, then her ears started slowly deflating, as though they'd got a puncture.

'Yes! It works!' I breathed out a huge sigh of relief and opened the fridge to get more ham. 'Let's give it to the teachers.'

'Hold on a second.' Anna slammed the fridge door in my face. 'Do you really think they're going to eat anything else that comes out of this kitchen?'

Before I had a chance to answer, a bloodcurdling scream came from the coach.

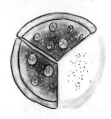

Chapter Six

'It's Mrs Heap,' said Anna.

'How d'you know?'

'That's exactly the noise she made when I brought in one of Useless's poos for Show and Tell.'

At the sound of her name Useless jumped up and down, tail wagging. Her ears had returned to their original size, and for a moment she looked completely normal. Well, normal for Useless.

My shoulders dropped and I grinned at Anna. 'It worked!'

But she didn't grin back. 'No, look. Her ears are still shrinking.'

In fact, her whole body was shrinking. As we watched, she shrank down to the size of a rabbit, and she showed no sign of stopping.

'You gave her too much,' cried Anna. 'If she carries

on like this she's going to disappear!'

We crouched down to look at her. She was now the size of a mouse. My heart was beating so loudly it sounded like a pair of trainers in the washing machine. *Thwack, thwack, thwack.* I tugged my fingers through my hair. *How was this happening?*

'She's going to fall through the floorboards!' wailed Anna.

I reached for a pizza box from the shelf. 'Quick! Put her in here.' Anna stroked her tiny head before I closed the box.

'*Arggghhhh!*' Another scream came from the coach. We poked our heads out of the kitchen so we could spy on the teachers again.

It was even worse than I'd imagined. Mr Gregson's wart was as large and lumpy as a cauliflower. Mr Shah's neck was so long, he had to bend over to avoid hitting the top of the coach. And Mrs Heap's eyes were bulging out of their sockets as though she'd had a terrible fright, which, I suppose, she had.

I gulped. 'What have we done?'

'What have *you* done, you mean.' Anna opened the pizza box and we both peered in. Useless had shrunk so much she looked like a furry beetle. 'Quick!' Anna grabbed the Grow bottle out of the briefcase. 'Let's give her some of this before she disappears into thin air.'

'What if she turns into Dumbo again?' I asked.

'I'll just give her one drop. You gave her two last time. It was too much.' Anna measured a drop onto a piece of ham and put it next to Useless in the pizza box. She scuttled towards it and took a miniscule nibble with her tiny jaws.

I knelt down to watch her, biting the edge of my

thumb. If Useless disappeared, Anna would never forgive me. I'd never forgive *myself*. I closed my eyes. *Please work. Please work. Please work.*

Anna clapped her hands. 'YES!'

I opened my eyes. Useless was swelling up, like a paddling pool being pumped up at speed. When she was back to her normal size she jumped off the table. Anna wrapped her arms around her, burying her face in her fur.

I let out a huge breath. 'One drop, that's the key! Where's that Shrink potion? We'll have to *force* it into the teachers' mouths, whether they like it or not!'

Suddenly Useless barked. A bright yellow flame shot out of her mouth, like a flame-throwing Stormtrooper.

I jumped back. 'Woah!'

She barked again. An even bigger flame flew out. She farted, knocked over two chairs and hid under the table.

Anna's eyes widened. 'What on earth—'

I leapt out of the way just before the next flame reached my legs and pulled Anna into the larder. Slamming the door behind us, we fell onto bags of flour.

'Are you sure you gave her the right one?' I asked, getting to my feet.

'I think so . . .'

I snatched the bottle from her. 'It says *Glow*, not Grow. What's wrong with your glasses?' I peered at it. 'There's something else. *'Use with extreme caution'*. Anna!'

'It's not my fault,' she muttered, taking her glasses off and glaring at them.

I rubbed my forehead, trying to think. 'Why did Useless get bigger when you gave it to her?'

'I dunno. Maybe the shrinking one wore off?'

I nodded. 'Yes, they wear off! That explains why we didn't see the spider – it had shrunk by the time we got up to the attic.'

Useless had stopped barking, so I gingerly opened the larder door. We found her cowering behind the service counter.

EXTERMINATE. EXTERMINATE. EXTERMINATE.

Help! It was my very loud *Doctor Who* ringtone.

Useless jumped up and down in circles, letting out a volley of howls. A series of flames tore out of her mouth, shooting to all corners of the shop. One of them scorched the wall, another set fire to the staircase.

'Make it stop!' cried Anna.

I picked up the phone from the counter. 'Dad?'

'I've just left Flowerdown, love. Back in ten minutes.' He paused. 'What's that barking? And crackling?'

'It's . . . a . . . a video game. Everything's fine.'

'Good.' He sighed. 'I've just spoken to the bank. I asked them to give us more time.'

My eyes darted to the flames licking the stairs. 'And?'

'They said no. We need to spend the next few days getting the shop ready to sell.'

A burning beam fell to the floor. At the same time, there was a crash of breaking glass as the window shattered, sending a swirling storm of flames and shards of glass into the shop.

Anna screamed and ducked behind the counter.

'Gotta go, Dad.' I hung up and stumbled through the smoke to get the briefcase from the kitchen.

'What are you doing?' asked Anna as I crouched down next to her with the briefcase. 'Let's get out of here! Call the fire parade!'

I was pretty sure that wasn't the right word, but this wasn't the moment to point it out. 'You go, I've got to fix this. It's my *home*. I can't just walk out and let it burn down.'

'I'm not leaving you on your own, butthead.'

Running my trembling fingers over the bottles, I tried to find something, anything, that could help. I picked up the bottle labelled *Wish*.

Anna rubbed her streaming eyes. 'You can't use that one.'

'But what if—'

'It literally says DO NOT USE! You'll die. Put it back!'

CRASH!

We poked our heads over the counter. Another beam had fallen to the shop floor. The smoke billowed towards us.

'Look!' shouted Anna, pointing outside. Through the smoke and flames appeared Mrs Winterbottom, crossing the road towards us. Anna gripped my arm. 'Look at her head!'

I gasped. Her head was enormous, the size of a space hopper, wobbling from side to side as she stepped up onto the pavement outside the shop. She opened the door but couldn't get any further – her head was jammed in the doorway. She roared like a trapped animal. 'Peter and Annabel, you are both expell—'

But we never heard the end of the sentence, because just then her head exploded. One minute it was there, the next it had gone.

I blinked.

This was bad. Very bad.

I unscrewed the cap of the Wish bottle.

Anna stared at me, eyes wide. 'You're not going to—'

'We've blown up Winterbotters, the shop's on fire and Dad's about to come home. I've got nothing to lose.' Lifting the bottle to my lips, I took a huge swig. The smoke was so thick and my eyes were stinging so much that I couldn't see a thing. I felt Anna slipping a hot hand into mine and Useless nudging between us.

'Go on then. Make a wish!' said Anna.

I closed my eyes. 'I wish we'd never found that briefcase.'

BOOM!

My eyes filled with a bright white light and we were thrown up into the air. The bottle flew out of my grip. It felt like a big hand had reached down and shaken the shop. Everything twisted then I blacked out.

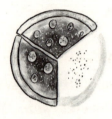

Chapter Seven

My eyelids flickered. Everything was so peaceful, so quiet.

Was I in *heaven*? At least I wouldn't have to see Archie Boyle again. There's no way he'd end up at the pearly gates.

I took a couple of sniffs. Surely heaven wouldn't smell this bad? I opened my eyes to find Useless's bottom inches from my face. Pushing her away, I sat up and looked around.

I gasped.

Then I clapped a hand to my mouth.

WHAAAAAAT?

The pizza shop was spotless. No swirling firestorm, no broken window, no headless headmistress. Anna was sprawled on her back by the counter, her eyes closed.

I jumped up and ran over to her. 'It worked! The wishing potion worked!'

She didn't move. Useless leapt on top of her, licking her face. Nothing. Useless looked at me then back at Anna, nuzzling her cheek.

I shook her by the shoulders. 'Anna? ANNA?'

Useless barked in her face. I flinched but no flames shot out of her mouth this time.

Anna opened one eye. 'So. Many. Questions.'

I grinned at her. 'You're alive! I thought the smoke—'

'What smoke?'

I ran to the window. The coach was still there, gleaming in the bright sunshine. The teachers were in their seats, looking totally normal. I spun around. My phone was on the counter, where I'd left it. Nothing was out of place. It was as though none of it had happened.

Im-poss-i-ble!

I let out the longest breath I've ever let out, feeling the tension release from my shoulders. That's when I noticed something shiny in the corner of the shop, near the window. I went closer. It was the Wish bottle, smashed to pieces. My heart sank. All those wishes I'd never be able to make. *I wish we could keep our home. I wish Fox Pizza would disappear.* And the biggest one of all. *I wish Mum were still alive.*

As I was picking up the jagged shards, Mrs Winterbottom strode around the back of the coach and marched towards the shop. Useless took one look at her and ran into the kitchen.

I threw the broken bottle in the bin and pulled Anna to her feet. 'She's alive! Look! Look at her head!'

Anna peered out of the window. 'What's so special about her head?'

'It's *there!*' I leapt forward to open the door and grinned at Mrs Winterbottom. It was a miracle. Not a wrinkle out of place. 'Welcome, Mrs Winterbottom. You're looking *wonderful*. Don't stand in the doorway. Come in!'

She narrowed her eyes at me as she stepped into the shop. 'What are you playing at, Peter?'

I beamed at her. 'I'm just really really *really* pleased to see you.' I wanted to hug her, but didn't think that would go down very well.

Anna was goggling at me like I was a five-headed alien.

Mrs Winterbottom pulled a purse out of her bag. 'I've come to pay you, yes?'

'Pay me?' I asked.

'Eighteen margheritas. Have you lost your mind?'

I blinked at her, my brain trying to keep up. Everything else must have happened as I remembered it, just without the potions; the coach had arrived, we'd made pizzas, the teachers had eaten them and no one had turned into a mutant!

Mrs Winterbottom cleared her throat. 'Why are you staring at me like I'm an exhibit in a museum, Peter?'

I couldn't exactly come out with *because I've seen the inside of your brain*, so I just went to the till to ring through the order.

She handed me her credit card. 'I'd like to tip you. Take three hundred pounds, yes? Everyone agreed the pizzas were the best they'd ever had, although they *were* on the small side.'

I caught Anna's eye and grinned as I took the payment. I'd never had such a big tip. Once I'd returned Mrs Winterbottom's card, she left. As the coach pulled away, the teachers on our side waved cheerily through the window.

Anna looked at me as we waved back. 'Now are you going to tell me what's going on?'

'What's the last thing you remember? Making pizzas?'

She looked blank.

'Finding something in the attic?' I asked.

Her face lit up. 'Yes! Useless was scratching the floorboards. What was it?'

'Hold on.' I ran upstairs, pulled down the attic steps and climbed up, bracing myself for a giant spider, but the web had completely disappeared. Finding the briefcase under the floorboard, in the exact place we'd found it that morning, I brought it down and opened it on the kitchen table. There was a gap where the wishing potion had been, but all the other bottles were there.

'Woah!' said Anna. 'What is it?'

It was like her memory had been erased, so I told her everything. Her eyes got bigger and bigger. When I got to the bit about Mrs Winterbottom's head exploding, she nearly fell off her stool. 'It didn't!'

'Right in the middle of expelling us. What are the chances?'

'How come you remember all this and I don't?' she asked.

'I dunno. Maybe because I drank the wishing potion?'

She puffed her cheeks out. 'I can't believe I missed all the fun. Can we do it again?'

I slammed the briefcase shut. 'No way. I'm going to bury these in the garden. They're dangerous.' I was about to take them out, when the shop door opened. I stuffed the briefcase into the cupboard under the sink just as Dad walked in.

He stopped dead, staring at Useless. 'You know dogs aren't allowed in here.'

'It's only Useless,' protested Anna.

'Even Useless,' he said.

Of course, he wanted to know how on earth we'd made three hundred pounds when we were meant to be closed, so I had to tell him the truth. OK, I left out a couple of minor details, like finding the potions and blowing up our headmistress. And I figured he wouldn't be too happy about the shop burning down, so I left that bit out too.

I chewed my thumb nail. 'Are you cross?'

He ran his eyes over the kitchen. 'You tidied up after yourselves, and they gave you a tip, so the pizzas can't have been too revolting.' He looked at me, eyes twinkling. 'How can I be cross?'

My heart lifted. 'Maybe we *will* make enough to save the shop after all.'

He ruffled my hair. 'You'll make a great pizza chef one day. But we need a lot more than three hundred pounds, love.'

That evening, Dad went to bed early to watch his

favourite programme – *The Great British Pizza-Off*.

I waited for it to get dark outside, then took the briefcase into the garden. It was a warm night. The light from the kitchen spilled onto the lawn. I glanced up at Dad's window – he'd closed his curtains.

There was a messy area in the back corner, deep in the shadows, where we put the compost and the mown grass. If I dug a hole over there, I was pretty sure Dad wouldn't notice it. Although it would have to be a big hole to fit the briefcase inside. Unless I took the potions out and buried them on their own?

I took a spade out of the shed, hoping Dad wouldn't hear the creaky door, and opened the briefcase. The first potion I picked up was the one labelled *Agility*.

I gazed at it. What would it do? Would it make me good at football? All the boys in my year played football, and some of the girls. Before school, at breaktime, after school. They were obsessed. I didn't get it. What was the point of running around after a ball? I'd much prefer to be inside with a slice of pizza and *Dragon Street*. But if I was *good* at it . . . My mind drifted. I imagined myself shooting an

impossible goal, everyone watching me. They'd go wild, screaming my name . . .

'Pete?' Dad was leaning out of his bedroom window. 'What are you doing?'

I leapt in front of the briefcase, hiding it from view. 'I heard a noise. I thought it was a . . . a . . . badger.'

'A badger?'

'I mean a burglar.'

He went still. 'I can't hear anything. Go to bed, love. We need to get up early tomorrow. I've got a list of properties to look at.'

I glared at him. 'We've still got three days.'

He shook his head. 'Just go to bed, love.'

'I'm not coming with you tomorrow!'

He closed his curtains and the room went dark.

I sighed. Earlier, I'd told him about my drone idea and he was like, 'don't be silly, drones cost thousands of pounds, and what if it crashed into a chimney or dropped a pizza on someone's head?' How on earth was I going to make ten thousand pounds in three days, without his help?

Just then the clouds parted and a shard of moonlight fell on the open briefcase, illuminating the bottles. My skin tingled. If that wasn't a sign, I didn't know what was. I almost expected a *dah dah daaah* from a majestic organ in the skies. Were these potions the answer I'd been looking for? And they'd been under my nose, or rather, over my head, all this time?

I put the spade away, went back inside, and called Anna.

She picked up straight away. 'Yup?'

'I've had an idea.'

She paused. 'Is it as rubbish as your other ideas?'

'It's . . . er . . . different. If we pull it off, we could save The Little Pizza Place *and* make it the coolest pizza shop in the entire universe. Which would make *me* the coolest boy in the entire universe.'

'Shut up.'

'And *you* the coolest girl in the entire universe.'

'Keep talking.'

'Everyone would ditch Fox Pizza and come flooding back . . . Anna? Hello?'

A minute later, Anna appeared at the shop door, wrapped in a blanket that had more holes than fabric. 'Where's your dad?'

'Shh! He's in bed.' I dragged her into the kitchen. Once she'd helped herself to a handful of biscuits, we sat down.

She stuffed a custard cream into her mouth. 'So?'

'You know how I was saying we needed to find some mind-blowing toppings to offer our customers?' I sat back, crossing my arms. 'I think we've found them.'

She looked around. 'Where?'

'Here!' I said, picking up the briefcase.

She snorted. 'Are you serious?'

'Deadly serious.'

'That wishing potion messed with your brain. You really think your dad's going to give these potions to your customers after what they did to Winterbotters?'

'He's not going to know.'

'WHAT?'

'Shh! We'll do it without him.'

She raised an eyebrow. 'How?'

'He's out all day tomorrow, so let's test them – work out what they all do.' I opened the briefcase and picked out one of the bottles. 'Look, *Flight*. Aren't you curious? Or this one, *Voice*. Or what about this one, *Invisibility*? Come on, it'll be fun.'

78

A little smile was playing on her lips. 'So, we test them. Then what?'

My cheeks were hot with excitement. 'We create a new menu full of crazy, magical pizzas. Can you imagine how popular we'd be? They'd be queuing around the block!'

'Where's your dad while all this is going on? Are you going to lock him in the attic?'

'I'll work something out. Now, are you going to help me or not?'

Her eyes shone. 'Of course I am, butthead.'

Chapter Eight

I was far too excited to sleep. Excited and hot. Having a pizza oven directly below my room was great in winter, not so great in summer.

Watching the minutes tick by on my TARDIS alarm clock, I played with the edge of my old camel wall-hanging, which Dad had picked up on holiday years ago. It had watched over me while I slept, every night since I was born.

If my plan worked, and it was a big *if*, I reckoned we could make ten thousand pounds in three days. Then we could pay the stupid bank back, and I'd never have to sleep anywhere apart from my cosy bedroom ever again.

I pushed the duvet off the bed and sprawled out on my back, a huge grin on my face. I must have eventually fallen asleep because before I knew it, the

Doctor's bossy voice was telling me to get up. *The time on planet Earth is six o'clock.*

Dad came into the bathroom, yawning, while I was brushing my teeth. 'You're up early,' he said.

I wiped my mouth on a towel and threw it at him. 'When are you off?'

'Are you coming with me?' He peered into the mirror, rubbing his chin. 'I'd like that – we are looking for our new home after all.' He caught my eye in the reflection. 'You'd get a tick on your chart.'

I smiled. 'I'd better stay here, just in case any more coachloads of hungry teachers turn up.'

He spun around to face me. 'Promise me you won't serve anyone until I get back.'

I swallowed. 'What about Anna? I made some dough for us last night.'

'OK, you can make pizzas for the two of you. But that's it. We'll lose our licence if anyone finds out a twelve-year-old is serving customers on their own.'

I nodded and went into my bedroom to get dressed. I definitely didn't want to lose our licence, whatever that was. At some point I'd have to get Dad on board. But first we had to test the potions.

Anna crossed the road, her guitar on her shoulder and Useless by her side, while I was taking the last pizza out of the oven. I went to open the door. 'Useless can't come in. Dad found a dog hair in the mozzarella last night and lost the plot.'

She scowled. 'Well I'm not leaving her on her own. Do you want me to help you or not?'

I paused. 'As long as she's out of here before Dad gets back.' I let them in and closed the blinds. Useless did an enormous fart and flashed a 'How dare you?' look at her bottom, before curling up in the corner of the shop.

I had butterflies in my stomach as I opened my laptop on the counter. 'I've set up an Excel spreadsheet. This column is for recording how much potion we use. This is for how long it lasts. And this is for how it changes us.'

Anna rolled her eyes. 'And you wonder why they call you a nerd.'

I took the Turbo potion out of the briefcase. 'I've ranked them in order of danger. This is the most harmless one I could find.'

'Turbo?'

'I'm guessing it'll make us faster.'

'Oh come on, try something a bit more fun, Captain Sensible. What about Invisibility? Or Flight?'

I glared at her. 'In case you've forgotten, we're doing this to save my home, not for *fun*. I've made a plan and I'm sticking to it.' I ran upstairs to get my dictionary and brought it back down.

'What's that for?' asked Anna, her eyebrow raised.

'I'm going to read it.' I flicked to the last page. 'It's got one thousand four hundred and sixty-two pages.' I waved the Turbo bottle in her face. 'Perfect way to test this!'

'You're reading the *dictionary*? What about running to London and back?'

'I CAN'T GO OUTSIDE.'

She put her hands up. 'OK, OK.'

I sliced one of the pizzas into eight, then squeezed a drop of potion onto one of the slices and took a bite. Anna pressed the stopwatch on her phone as I opened the dictionary, turned to the first page and read out loud. 'A, a . . .'

'Get on with it. We'll both be dead before you get to the Bs.'

I sped up. 'Aardvark, aardwolf, Aaron's beard, Aaron's rod, aasvogel—'

'It's not working. Can you feel anything?'

I shook my head and had another bite of pizza, with another drop of potion. I picked up the dictionary again. When I got to 'abacus', my skin went all tingly and my brain fizzed like sherbet. My tongue started tripping over the words so fast, I had to stop reading out loud. I finished the first page, then the next and the next. My fingers could hardly turn the pages fast enough. Before I knew it, I'd reached the last word:

'Zyzzyva'. I felt exhausted, like my brain had run a hundred marathons.

Anna was staring at me with her mouth open. 'Were you properly reading it? Or just turning the pages?'

I was so stunned, I could hardly think straight. 'I *think* I read it all.'

She picked up the dictionary and opened it randomly.

'Hold on.' I laughed nervously. 'I'm not going to remember every—'

'*Clatterfart*. What does clatterfart mean?'

I blinked. 'It's an old Tudor word for a gossip.'

Anna checked the dictionary then narrowed her eyes at me. 'Beginner's luck. How about this one: *humpenscrump*.'

'A musical instrument.'

'There's no way you'll get this one. *Hippopotomonstrosesquipedaliophobic.*'

'Someone who's fearful of long words,' I said, without even thinking.

She looked up, her eyes sparkling. 'You remembered *every* word!' She peered at the label on the Turbo bottle. 'They should have put *Photographic Memory* on here too.'

My mind boggled with possibilities. 'I'm going to memorise all the famous moves on Chess.com. I'll be a grandmaster by the time I'm thirteen!' But as I spoke, I realised the tingles had disappeared. I felt normal again. 'I think it's worn off. Try another word.'

'Pakapoo.'

I closed my eyes and tried to remember. Nothing. 'It's gone.'

Anna stopped the stopwatch. 'That's annoying. I was going to use it to learn my lyrics for this new song I'm playing with the band.' She reached into the briefcase and pulled out the Flight bottle. 'This one next.'

'No, no, no. Intelligence is number two, not Flight.' I pushed my laptop towards her and pointed at the spreadsheet.

But it was too late. She'd already measured a drop of the Flight potion onto a slice of pizza and taken a bite before I could stop her.

I threw my hands in the air. 'What if you crash into the ceiling?'

'Stop worrying and start the stopwatch!' She leapt around the shop, flapping her arms. Useless chased after her, barking.

'What are you doing?' I asked.

'I'm flying!'

'No, you're not. You're jumping and flapping your arms.'

'Give me some more then.'

I measured out one more drop of Flight potion for her. This time when she bounded across the floor she was extra bouncy, as if she had a pogo stick.

'Look at me!' She bounced around the room in a circle then headed towards me, Useless snapping at her heels.

'Watch out!' I yelled as she came closer, showing no sign of stopping.

Just before she reached me, she pushed off the ground with one foot and took off, almost brushing my chin with her boot as she skimmed over my head.

I clapped a hand to my mouth as she made a quick turn to avoid the wall. How was this possible? Anna was *flying*. She was swimming breaststroke, *through the air*.

'Wah!' she cried, as she flew in circles around the room. 'I'm a bird!'

Shivers skittered down my spine. These potions were mad. Extraordinary. Out of this world.

'There's not enough space in here,' she said. 'Can I go outside? To the end of the road and back?'

'No!' I shouted, blocking the door.

'I'll go upstairs then.' And before I could stop her, she flew up the stairs, knocking a couple of photos off the wall. Useless ran after her, barking. I heard Anna crashing around, bumping into things.

'Come back down!' I shouted.

'I'm trying to turn around,' she called out, over the sound of breaking glass. 'Your dad didn't like that boat picture, did he?' She suddenly shot head first down the stairs, chased by Useless. She hovered in the air for a second, then collapsed like a sack of flour.

Chapter Nine

Useless jumped on top of Anna and licked her face. Anna pushed her off and grinned at me. 'That was amazing! I'm doing it again.'

'No! We can't use it all up.' I tapped the results into the laptop. 'Two drops. Flight time three minutes and forty seconds.'

She clambered to her feet and pulled another bottle out of the briefcase. 'What do you think this one does – *Replication*?' Her eyes lit up. 'Do you think it will make two of me?'

I plucked it out of her hand. 'A, it's my turn. B, that one's at the bottom of the list. And . . . C, even when it's your turn and we get to the bottom of the list, you're not testing it.'

'Why not?'

'Because the thought of two of you makes me want to gouge my eyes out.'

'I'll pretend I didn't hear that.' Grabbing the bottle, she squeezed a drop onto a slice of pizza.

'Give it here!' I shouted, chasing her around the shop.

'Too late!' She shoved the pizza into her mouth.

Grumbling, I started the stopwatch, wondering how the Replication potion was going to work. Would she split in two like an amoeba? Or would she turn into a shimmering avatar, like in a video game?

Tap tap. I spun around as someone tapped my shoulder.

'Boo!' It was Anna, behind me. She stuck her tongue out.

I turned back. Anna was also in front of me, her mouth wide open at the sight of her identical twin. It was *very* weird. The potion had created an exact replica of Anna. A clone. It had just appeared, out of thin air. I twisted around again. The two Annas had the same glasses, the same purple cardigan, the same Doc Martens.

Useless's hackles shot up. She let out a low growl,

looking from one Anna to the other, then backed into the kitchen, barking.

Anna pointed at her double. 'You're me!'

The other Anna grinned. She was chewing the sleeve of her cardigan. 'No, you're me!'

I put my head in my hands. This was a nightmare. When I looked up – it can't have been more than a second later – there were four of them. Four identical Annas. It was impossible to tell which was the real one.

One of them opened the briefcase. 'Where's that potion? Let's make more of us.'

'Absolutely not!' I dragged her away from the briefcase and pushed her into the kitchen. But when I turned back, another one was merrily squeezing Replication potion all over the pizza. I snatched the bottle from her and looked for somewhere to hide the briefcase.

Thwack! Something hit the back of my head. I spun around.

Conk! A lemon bounced off my nose.

Clutching the briefcase to my chest, I went into the kitchen. One of the Anna clones was in the larder, throwing handfuls of flour over her shoulder. Another one was juggling fruit. Squashed bananas and bruised apples littered the floor. Ducking to avoid an orange, I poked my head out of the kitchen.

My stomach did a massive flip.

How many were there? Thirty? Forty? Too many to count, that's for sure. Some of them were playing Frisbee with pizza boxes. One of them was sliding down the stairs on . . . I peered closer . . . my Doctor Who duvet!

That was it. I climbed onto the counter, pushing two Anna clones off to make space. Putting the briefcase between my legs, I cupped my hands around my mouth and shouted 'Enough!'

Everyone ignored me.

This was impossible. Where was Anna when I needed her? I clapped my hands together. 'Will the real Anna – my friend – show herself?'

'I'm the real Anna!'

I jumped. 'Who said that?'

'Me!' said a girl pressed into the corner by the door.

'No, she's not. I'm the real Anna!' said another one, leaning over the banisters.

Someone grabbed my ankle. 'I really *am* Anna, I promise!' She put her hand on the briefcase. 'Give us another potion.'

'Come on, Captain Sensible,' said the girl next to her, trying to open the clasps.

'Get off!' As I kicked their hands away, I heard a familiar sound coming from the kitchen.

Woof!

Useless! Surely she'd be able to sniff out the real Anna? I jumped off the counter with the briefcase and squeezed my way into the kitchen. It looked like there'd been a snowstorm. Everything was covered in flour, including Useless, who was barking at the larder door. She looked like a tiny polar bear.

'Good girl, Useless!' I shoved one of the clones to the side to open the larder door. Useless squeezed through.

'Close it!' hissed a voice from the depths of the larder.

I went in and quickly pulled the door shut. Two eyes, wide with terror, gleamed back at me from behind a sack of flour.

'Anna! What are you doing in here?' I pushed the flour to one side and knelt down. Useless wriggled past me and leapt up on her, shaking flour everywhere.

She sneezed, then stroked Useless's white furry face. 'Am I really like that?'

'Like what?'

She nodded her head towards the door. The noise

in the kitchen was louder than ever. 'Them. You know . . . a bit . . .'

'Hectic?' I offered. 'Yes . . . I mean, no. Well . . . sometimes.'

She buried her head in Useless's fur.

I squeezed her shoulder. 'Imagine if there were gazillions of me, it would be *awful*.'

'Awful,' she repeated, in a muffled voice.

'I'M SQUASHED!' shouted one of the Annas in the kitchen.

'LET'S GO OUTSIDE!' called another.

'No!' I pushed the latch, imagining hundreds of identical girls spilling out of our shop. But I couldn't open the door. 'Help!'

Anna stood up and we both shoved the door as hard as we could, but it wouldn't budge. We were trapped by the sheer number of Annas in the kitchen.

I quickly opened the briefcase. 'There's got to be something . . . yes!' I pulled out the Strength potion and unscrewed the cap. 'I'll break us out of here!'

There was a loud thump on the door and Anna jumped, knocking the bottle out of my hand. The potion dripped through a big gap in the floorboards.

'Anna!' Picking up the bottle, I peered into it. It was empty, apart from a thin sheen of liquid coating the inside of the bottle. I grabbed the Replication potion from the briefcase. 'Do you think we could use this to make more Strength potion?'

Anna shook her head. 'The potions only work on people and dogs.' She paused. 'And possibly spiders.'

'STREET PARTY!' yelled one of the Annas in the kitchen. 'CONGA TO THE DOOR!'

Anna's face lit up. 'Ooh, that sounds fun.'

I glared at her and squeezed a drop of the Replication potion into the Strength bottle, then put it on the shelf. We both stared at it. Nothing happened.

'Told you,' said Anna.

I put my head in my hands.

'CONGA, CONGA, CON-GA! CONGA, CONGA, CON-GA!'

'Um . . . Pete?'

I looked up to see the Strength bottle filling up, as if an invisible jug was pouring liquid into it. 'It worked!'

'Quick! It might disappear when the Replication potion wears off,' said Anna.

I measured a drop of the new Strength potion onto my tongue. My body vibrated, gently at first, but increasingly violently, like an electric shock was coursing through my blood. A strange swelling sensation spread across my body. I lifted my hands. The veins were bulging, as if fat blue worms were squirming around under my skin.

Anna made a face. 'Eww! Are you OK?'

'Do I *look* OK?'

'CONGA, CONGA, CON-GA!'

My clothes were getting tighter and tighter. I felt like I was being squeezed like a tube of toothpaste. I managed to pull my hoodie over my head but my T-shirt underneath was too tight to take off.

'I can't breathe!' I gasped.

Anna pulled the neck of my T-shirt. 'Does this help?'

'Arghh! You're cutting off my airways!' I grabbed the bottom of the T-shirt with both hands. To my surprise it ripped in two as easily as paper. Taking a gulp of air, I looked down at my huge, muscular hands in astonishment.

Anna's eyes were as round as pepperoni. 'All right,

Superman. Get out there and show them who's boss.'

I opened the larder door with my index finger, knocking over clones like dominoes, and barged my way through the kitchen into the shop.

My heart did a flip-flop.

A conga line of Annas was streaming out of the door into the sunshine outside. 'CONGA, CONGA, CON-GA!'

I pushed past the conga line and poked my head out of the door. There were about a hundred clones conga-ing down Harwood Road. Mrs Afolabi was at the postbox on the corner, rummaging through her bag. If she looked up now, she'd probably have a heart attack.

'Annas!' I hissed. 'Get inside! Now!'

One of them looked at me. 'Why should we?'

'Biscuits.' Anna appeared next to me, waving a packet of chocolate Hobnobs. 'Come and get 'em!'

That got their interest. They piled back into the shop, climbing over each other to get closer to Anna, who was now on the counter, pelting Hobnobs out faster than a machine gun.

Mrs Afolabi looked up, her mouth forming a perfect

'O' as I squeezed the last few Annas into the shop. I put a finger to my lips and pulled the door closed. Thank goodness for the blinds.

I turned around to see Anna holding an empty packet. 'Sorry. All gone.'

'Nooooo!' shouted the clone next to me.

'Don't blame me,' said Anna. 'Pete never has enough biscuits.'

'Back outside! CONGA, CONGA, CON-GA!' The clone reached for the door handle, so I put my arm out to stop her. She went flying. I winced, anticipating the landing, but she never hit the ground. She just disappeared in mid-air.

'It's wearing off!' I shouted. Another one tried to crawl between my legs, but I lifted her up as if she were a doll and threw her to one side. She also popped out of existence before she landed. As I fended the clones off they gradually disappeared, one after the other, until no one was left.

'Good job!' Anna jumped off the counter and put her hand up for a high five. When I hit it, she flew backwards, landing on her bottom. 'Ouch!'

'Sorry! I forgot.'

She got to her feet and kicked her boot against the edge of the counter. 'Pete?'

'Yup?'

She looked up. 'Stick to the spreadsheet.'

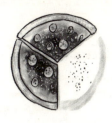

Chapter Ten

We quickly worked our way through the rest of the potions. I tested some, Anna tested some, and there were a few we both *had* to try. The only one we didn't test was the Glow potion. Burning the shop down once was bad, twice would just be irresponsible.

When we'd finished, the Excel spreadsheet looked like this:

Potion	Number of drops	Duration	Effect
Turbo	2	1 min 42	**Pete:** *I read and remembered the entire dictionary (1,462 pages).*
	2	1 min 48	**Anna:** I ran around the counter 3,000 times.
			Pete: *Actually 2,793 times (I watched it back on slo-mo).*
Flight	2	1 min 30	**Anna:** WOW! I flew all over the house!
			Pete: *Excellent for changing lightbulbs.*
			NB: Remember to close doors/windows.
Replication	?	Too long	**Anna:** No comment.
			Pete: *One Anna is more than enough.*
			NB: Don't use.
Strength	1	2 min 29	**Pete:** *I got stronger, broke us out of the larder and saved the day.*
			Anna: You definitely smelled stronger.
Intelligence	1	2 min 52	**Pete:** *I completed a Sixth Form Maths paper that I found online. Highlight of the day.*
			Anna: You forgot to show your workings.
			Pete: *I did it in my head.*
			Anna: B+

Potion	Number of drops	Duration	Effect
Voice	2	2 min 16	**Anna:** I hit some super-high notes. Must try it with the band. **Pete:** *It's a miracle no windows cracked.*
Agility	3	2 min 31	**Pete:** *I did 126 keepy-uppies while doing a handstand!* **Anna:** Never thought I'd say this, but I'm impressed.
Animal	2	2 min 50	**Anna:** A-ma-zing! I turned into a fox.
	2	2 min 44	**Pete:** *Hmmm. I turned into a butterfly.* **Anna:** I think it changes you into your spirit animal. **Pete:** *I don't.*
Grow	1	2 min 05	**Anna:** I turned into a giant. Sorry about the hole in the ceiling. NB: Affects people/dogs/spiders differently.
Shrink	1	2 min 28	**Pete:** *I shrank down to 3.5 cm – same size as Luke and Han. Useless looked like a huge, hairy dinosaur.*
	1	2 min 24	**Anna:** My head shrank down to the size of a tennis ball. Everything else stayed the same. NB: Don't take too much – you might disappear completely.
Invisibility	1	3 min	Epic game of hide and seek.
Laughter	2	3 min 55	**Pete:** *My tummy's still hurting.*
	2	3 min 50	**Anna:** Me too!

'I think we're missing one,' said Anna, running her finger down the first column.

I peered into the briefcase. 'Shapeshifter. We'll have to do it later – Dad's going to be back soon.'

'Oh come on. It won't take long.'

'OK. But you test it. I'll be sick if I have any more pizza.'

Anna picked the bottle out. 'What do you think it does?'

'I reckon it can turn you into anything you want.'

'Like a vampire, or a werewolf?'

I blinked. 'How about something a bit less terrifying that won't try to eat me?'

She adjusted her glasses and nodded.

'Have you thought of something?' I asked.

'Yup. Wish me luck.' She measured a drop of potion onto the pizza and took a bite.

I smiled nervously. 'Go on then, tell me what it is.'

But she was gone. One minute she was there, the next she'd vanished into thin air.

'Anna?' The shop was totally empty apart from me and Useless. She hadn't turned into anything.

Unless . . .

I bent down and looked at the pizzas on the counter. Was there an extra one? I poked the top one, wondering if it would . . . I don't know . . . talk to me?

A flash of brown scampered across the floor.

I knelt down. A tiny mouse was under the counter, nibbling a crust of pizza. 'Anna? You're a *mouse*?'

It looked straight into my eyes and gave me The Look.

'It *is* you!' I lay down on the floor and put my hand out towards it. 'You're so sweet! Jump up!'

A furry paw suddenly shot out from the other side of the counter. The mouse disappeared.

'Useless!' I screamed. I ran around the counter to find her lying on her tummy, a tiny tail dangling from her mouth.

She held my gaze for a few seconds, then swallowed. I yanked her jaws apart but it was too late. Anna had gone. An hour ago there'd been a hundred Annas, now there were none.

I felt dizzy and grabbed hold of the counter for support. Useless nuzzled my leg and I pushed her away, but then I felt bad. It wasn't her fault. I put my hand out and she licked it which made me feel icky so I stroked her head instead.

Just then a key turned in the door. I shoved Useless and the briefcase into the loo under the stairs, as Dad came in.

'I've brought someone to see you.' He frowned. 'Why did you close the blinds?'

I picked up the rest of the pizzas and took them into the kitchen, so he couldn't see my face. He always knew, just by looking at me, what I was feeling. 'Too bright,' I shouted, over my shoulder.

'The sunlight was hurting my . . . um . . . eyes.'

Dad was opening the blinds as I came back out. 'What sunlight? It's cloudy.'

'Did you say someone's here?' I asked quickly, changing the subject.

'Granny Tortoise. She wanted to see us here, one last time.'

I looked out of the window. Granny was sitting in the passenger seat of the car. 'Is she . . . dying?'

He laughed. 'No! We're moving out in three days, remember?'

I rubbed my ear. 'Oh yeah.'

He went to help Granny out of the car. She gripped her Zimmer frame with both hands. She must have been straight once, but ever since I could remember, she'd been curled up like a Quaver. She was slower than when I'd last seen her. It took her about two minutes just to cross the pavement.

I crouched down and hugged her when she reached the shop. She smelled of hot water bottles, and felt as fragile as a butterfly.

She took a dry, papery hand off her frame and clutched my wrist tightly. 'What's wrong, dear?'

I felt a lump in my throat. How could she tell? She was so hunched over, she could hardly see my face. 'Nothing,' I said, as I helped her through to the kitchen.

She grunted as she collapsed into a chair at the kitchen table. 'Where's that lovely friend of yours?'

'Yes, where's Anna?' asked Dad.

My mind was racing. What was I going to tell them? *Anna's in the dog.* They'd never believe me. As I was trying to work out what to say, Dad went towards the downstairs loo.

'No!' I shouted, as he turned the handle. 'I mean . . . there's no loo roll.'

'And you didn't think about replacing it?' he grumbled, going upstairs.

As soon as he'd gone, a scrabbling noise came from the downstairs loo. My heart lifted. Perhaps Anna had turned back into a human and burst out of Useless? Maybe she'd been squeezed out as the world's most awkward poo?

Granny had her back to me in the kitchen and Dad was still upstairs, so I opened the loo door an inch. But it was just Useless, scratching the door. Her ears were pulled back and she looked at me with big, sad eyes. I opened the door a bit further so I could stroke behind her ears. 'You're missing her too, aren't you?' I whispered.

'Missing who?' whispered a voice right behind me.

I spun around, straight into Anna. Useless pushed past me and jumped up, her tail wagging so hard it looked like it was going to fall off. I threw my arms around both of them. I couldn't help myself.

Anna pushed me away. 'Get off!'

'Peter?' called Granny, from the kitchen. 'Can I help myself to—'

'Go for it, Granny!' I pulled Anna behind the counter, away from the kitchen door. 'How on earth did you get out?' I whispered.

She looked totally blank.

'Useless ate you!' I pointed under the counter. 'You were there, nibbling pizza, and Useless ate you.'

'What are you talking about?' she said.

'You turned into a mouse!'

She made a face. 'No I didn't. I hate mice!'

'That's exactly the look the mouse gave me!'

She shook her head. 'I turned into a pizza. I wanted to see what it felt like.'

I glanced at the pizzas on the counter. 'I knew it! What *did* it feel like?'

'Cheesy. Can I try something else? A cat? Then I can eat the mouse.'

'I told you, Useless ate the mouse.'

Dad came down the stairs. 'What's all this about mice?' He stopped on the bottom step when he saw Useless. His face went beetroot. '*What* did I tell you about Useless?'

'Don't be cross. She just caught a mouse,' I said, nudging Anna. 'Didn't she?'

'She did.' Anna wiped a finger along the counter and peered at it. 'This place is filthy. You'd be overrun with mice if it weren't for Useless.'

I could tell Dad was struggling with this. He didn't know whether to be angry or grateful. In the end, he settled with a chuckle. 'Maybe we should change her name to Useful.'

Just then, we heard Granny's voice coming from the kitchen. 'Delicious pizza, dear.'

Anna and I stared at each other, then I ran next door, my heart jackhammering in my chest.

Chapter Eleven

The plate of pizzas we'd used for testing was on the kitchen table. I couldn't remember which ones had potion on. Granny had a slice in her hand – she was about to take another bite.

I snatched it from her. 'Sorry, you can't have that.'

'Pete! What are you doing?' said Dad.

'I was enjoying that!' Granny grumbled. Suddenly her whole body vibrated, like she'd had a huge electric shock. Her eyes shot wide open then they closed, and she went completely still. It looked like she'd fallen asleep.

Dad ran to put his arm around her. 'Not another funny turn.'

I looked at Anna. 'I'm not sure it's a funny turn, Dad.'

'I don't know *what* you call it but I'm calling an ambulance,' he said.

While he was getting his phone from next door, Granny's eyes shot open again and her head started ratcheting up, lifting higher and higher as her neck unfurled. She took my hand. 'Peter?'

I gulped. *Which potion had she had?*

'Goodness me!' said Granny, leaping out of her chair. Her neck was now completely straight. She was taller than all of us. 'I haven't felt this good in years!' She put her hands on her hips and kicked her legs in the air, whooping with excitement.

'Agility,' Anna and I said in unison.

I turned to see Dad frozen to the spot, his phone to his ear. 'Er . . . sorry . . . cancel that.' He put the phone down and rubbed his eyes. They were as wide as saucers. 'What the . . .'

Granny was cartwheeling around the kitchen table. 'Listen, Dad—'

He put his hand up. 'This is a miracle!'

Granny stretched her arms up and touched her toes. 'Ha! I've never been able to do that.'

I winced. 'Be careful!'

'Be careful? I've been careful all my life. I'm bored of being careful! Stuck in that dreadful place all day, it's suffocating. I'm finally free!' She skipped out of the kitchen, like a little child, Useless chasing after her.

'A miracle!' repeated Dad, as we followed Granny to the front of the shop. I quickly closed the blinds again.

She crouched down facing the window, then jumped, driving her knees up to her chin and flipping her whole body over in a backflip. Then she leapt onto the counter and did a front walk-over, a back walk-over, a front flip and a flip-flop.

That's when I noticed her head was slightly bent forward. The potion was wearing off. I ran up to the counter. 'Granny, time to come down.'

'One last move! The Thomas Salto – I saw it on telly once. It was banned in the Olympics for being too dangerous.'

'Absolutely not,' shouted Dad, pointing a wooden spoon at her. 'Get down!'

'You'll break your back!' I yelled.

'Don't do it!' said Anna.

'Too late!' Granny winked at us, then closed her eyes. And jumped.

I watched through my fingers as she did two somersaults in the air whilst twisting her body around. She landed in a perfect forward roll, but as she hit the floor there was an ominous CRACK.

'Granny!' I wailed, crouching down next to her. Her eyes were shut and she was completely still.

'What was that noise?' asked Anna, with a trembling voice. 'Her neck?'

I was shaking so much I couldn't talk. *Had I killed Granny Tortoise?*

'It might have been . . . this,' said Dad. We spun around to see him holding half a wooden spoon in each hand. He must have snapped it in two. 'What? It was tense.'

I let out a deep breath, just as Granny opened her eyes and beamed at me. 'Can I have another one, dear?'

It was late by the time Dad got back from Flowerdown. He stormed into the kitchen. 'Well?'

I glanced at Anna but she had her head down, strumming her guitar. Useless was curled up by her feet.

I coughed. 'I was trying to come up with a way to sell more pizzas, so we wouldn't be homeless and . . . um . . . I told you I was thinking about using . . . er . . . drones to deliver them, and so . . . um . . . me and Anna . . . I mean Anna and I . . .'

Anna rolled her eyes and put her guitar down. 'We found some weird potions in the attic and decided to use them as pizza toppings, but one of them must have spilled onto Granny Tortoise's pizza.'

Dad took a deep breath, closed his eyes and ran his hands through his hair. I looked down at my feet. I suppose it could have been worse. At least Anna didn't say anything about Mrs Winterbottom or the fire.

She clicked her fingers. 'Oh, and I almost forgot. One of the potions blew up Winterbotters and another one turned Useless into this mutant fire-dog and she nearly burnt the shop down.'

'Anna!' I said, through gritted teeth.

'Then Pete took this wishing potion that nearly killed us but actually it sorted everything out.' She smiled brightly. 'So it's all good.'

I put my hood over my head and pulled the strings tight, waiting for Dad to lose the plot.

There was silence. Then a snort of laughter, then a chuckle.

I pushed my hood off and looked at Anna nervously.

Dad exploded in a proper belly laugh, rocking backwards and forwards, tears rolling down his cheeks.

'So . . . you're not cross?' I asked. 'I feel bad about Granny Tortoise. That was not part of the plan.'

His smile snapped out like a light. 'OK, who's going to tell me what really happened?'

I looked at Anna then back at Dad. 'It sounds crazy, but it's exactly like Anna said.'

He huffed. 'You've been playing too many video games. Your heads are full of nonsense.'

'I'm serious, Dad. How else do you explain what happened to Granny?'

He stared at me. 'So where are these *potions*, then?'

I went to get the briefcase from the downstairs loo and opened it on the kitchen table.

Dad's eyes widened as he ran his fingers over the labels. 'Where did you say you found them?'

'In the attic, under the floorboards.'

'Actually, Useless found them,' Anna said proudly.

Dad picked up one of the bottles and held it up to the light, while I pulled out the snippet of newspaper.

'Look at this.' I pointed at the photo. 'Did she live here before us?'

He took the article from me. 'Professor Silva Tregoning. Yes, that rings a bell. I never met her though.'

'What did she have in her shop?' I asked. 'Was it a chemist?'

Dad shook his head. 'There wasn't a shop here when we bought it. It was a house. We converted it.'

'So why did she leave these behind?' asked Anna.

'No idea.' He looked at the bottles again. 'You want me to believe that one of these made Granny do all those backflips?'

I picked out the Agility potion. 'This one.'

He took it from me, opened it and sniffed. 'Must be some sort of vitamin mix. Granny had an extreme reaction to it, probably because it's so old.'

I frowned. 'We've tested them. They're not vitamins. They all change you in different ways. *Really* change you.'

'Try one, if you don't believe us,' said Anna. 'Put a drop on your tongue.'

Dad snorted and picked up a bottle. He tried to hide the label but I caught a glimpse: *Shrink*.

'Please, not that one,' I said. 'It's freaky. It shrank Anna's head.'

'Utter nonsense,' he muttered, measuring a couple of drops onto his tongue.

'One drop!' I said.

'Too late,' said Anna.

Dad handed the bottle to me. 'Nothing's happening. See?'

'Be patient, Dad. It takes a couple of minutes.'

But perhaps because he'd taken two drops, within seconds his shirt, normally stretched tight over his middle, was loose and flappy. His eyes almost popped out of their sockets.

'Now do you believe us?' I asked.

He lifted his shirt and we watched his big, round tummy disappearing in front of our eyes, until it was as flat as an ironing board. 'It's t . . . it's t . . .' he spluttered.

I bit my knuckles, wondering what he was going to say. *It's terrifying? It's twisted? It's time to call the ambulance back?*

His face lit up. 'It's tremendous! Look at me! I'm eighteen again!' He pulled his shirt sleeves up. His arms, normally as thick as branches, were long and slender. As we watched they got thinner and thinner, until they looked like hairy twigs, thin enough to snap. It was quite disturbing, seeing my cuddly dad turn into a stick insect. He looked up nervously. 'How do I stop it?'

'You can't,' I said. 'You just have to wait for it to wear off. That's why we've been testing them, to work out how much you need. One drop is enough for most of them.'

'Two drops was probably about right for you though,' said Anna. 'No offence.'

But Dad was too busy gawping at his new, skinny body to take offence. 'This is unbelievable!'

I felt my shoulders drop. It was such a relief finally telling him the truth.

He ran his hands over his face, which was looking more skeletal by the second. 'My double chin! It's gone!' He went into the downstairs loo and turned on the light, leaving the door open so we could see him admiring himself in the mirror.

'So . . . what do you think about our idea?' I said.

'Your idea,' said Anna. 'I'm just here for the free pizza.'

'Hmm?' Dad turned around and lifted his shirt to see his back.

'We use the potions to create a brand new menu full of extraordinary pizzas,' I said. 'A pizza that makes you fly, or laugh, or super clever. I reckon we'll make enough money in three days – well, two days now – to save the shop. What do you think?'

Dad dropped his shirt and we followed him into the kitchen. He looked at the potions. 'You really think this is going to work, love?'

'I really do,' I said.

'Then what?'

'We put them back where we found them and never touch them again.'

He stood back, folding his twig arms. 'I can't tell if this is the best idea in the world or the absolute worst.'

I shrugged. 'What have we got to lose?'

He slowly nodded, a huge smile spreading across his face. 'Let's go for it.'

Chapter Twelve

I blinked groggily at the clock, my eyes stinging with tiredness. Six o'clock in the morning. Dad was brushing his teeth, then he went downstairs, whistling. I couldn't remember the last time I'd heard him whistling.

'Morning!' he called, emerging from the kitchen in a cloud of flour as I came down. He peered at me from underneath his bandana. 'You look like you need Dad's hot chocolate.'

Dad made the *best* hot chocolate. Instead of cocoa powder, his secret was to melt dark and milk chocolate into hot milk. Then he piled a mountain of whipped cream, mini marshmallows and chocolate shavings on top.

I sat at the kitchen table, my hands wrapped around a steaming mug, while Dad made the dough, and we talked about our plan for the day. This is what we decided:

1. Rather than serving whole pizzas, we would serve one slice at a time, each with the appropriate dose of potion.
2. We would only serve margherita pizzas, with a potion topping.
3. We would charge £20 for a slice of pizza. It was a lot, but we thought it was worth it.
4. We would only serve one customer or family at a time, to avoid total mayhem.
5. If we ran out of any potion, we could use the Replication potion to make more.

I felt a million times better once I'd finished my hot chocolate. Dad got the stepladder out and I climbed up to scrub the old menu off the chalkboard above the counter. We had fun coming up with silly names for the new pizzas, and I wrote them up on the board.

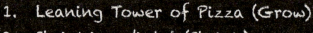

1. Leaning Tower of Pizza (Grow)
2. Shrinking Violet (Shrink)
3. Paws 'n' Pizza (Animal)
4. Morpharella (Shapeshifter)
5. The Need for Speed (Turbo)
6. Pizza Pan (Flight)
7. Muscles and Mozzarella (Strength)
8. Where the Olive are You? (Invisibility)
9. Cheesy Chuckles (Laughter)
10. Smarto Tomato (Intelligence)
11. Mozzarella-la-la-la (Voice)
12. Pizza the Action (Agility)

'I've been thinking about our name – The Little Pizza Place,' said Dad, as I climbed down the ladder.

'Maybe we should change it to something that gives a better idea of what we're offering.'

'The Magical Pizza Place?'

He wrinkled his nose.

'Listen,' I said. 'We've got a pizza that makes you fly, another one that makes you invisible, another one that turns you into an animal. If that's not magic, I don't know what is.'

He couldn't argue with that. I painted the word 'Magical' onto a piece of wood and Dad nailed it over the word 'Little' on the sign outside, while I arranged the potions neatly on a shelf next to the till.

'Dad?' I asked, when he came back in.

'Hmm?'

I rubbed the back of my neck. 'How about we stop doing deliveries and offer eat-in only. Just to keep our customers safe, of course. Could be dangerous if we let them loose before the potion's worn off.'

He frowned. 'Where's everyone going to sit?'

I'd thought about this. 'We could bring our kitchen table out here. It'll fit along that wall, and there'll still be lots of room.'

He eyed up the space. 'Let's try it.'

We carried the kitchen table through into the shop and pushed it against the far wall, arranging the chairs around it. I let out a huge breath. No more deliveries! This was working out even better than I'd imagined.

Dad peered out of the window. 'It's very quiet out there today. End of July . . . I suppose lots of people are on holiday. How many slices of pizza did you say we have to sell?'

'Four hundred and eighty-five slices in two days,' I replied. 'It's fine, Dad. As soon as the first customers try these pizzas, they'll tell their friends, who'll tell their friends, who'll tell *their* friends.'

'But how do we get the first customers in the door?' Dad rubbed his chin. 'Social media?'

'I think you need *friends* on social media for that to work.' My heart sank. I hadn't thought about it but Dad had a very good point. How were we going to tell people about our new menu?

Just then, Anna burst in with Useless. She thrust a pile of bright orange sheets of paper into my hand. 'I made flyers.'

A lump appeared in my throat as I flicked through them. They must have taken her ages.

WELCOME TO THE
MAGICAL PIZZA PLACE!
* 121 HARWOOD ROAD * *

* STEP INSIDE FOR *
* A MAGICAL EXPERIENCE! *

'I saw the new sign from my bedroom window.' She grinned at me. 'Let's go and hand them out. Spread the word.' She must have seen the doubt on my face, because she grabbed my arm. 'Come on. It'll be fun!'

'What, now?'

'Yes, now!' She checked the time. 'It's ten o'clock.'

'Ten o'clock?' Dad spun around to look at the clock on the wall. 'Help!' He rushed into the kitchen.

'Just the two of us then,' said Anna. 'Let's go.'

I gulped. If ever there was a time to break a promise,

it was now. I ran upstairs to get Luke Skywalker and Han Solo, and stuffed them in my pocket. When I came back down, Anna's smile was gone.

'I've got band practice,' she said. 'I completely forgot.'

'You can't go. Not now.'

She paused. 'You start without me. I'll be as quick as I can.'

My heart started pounding. 'Great. So I'm on my own.'

She put her hands on my trembling shoulders. 'You can do it, I know you can. You're stronger than you think.'

I blinked. I didn't feel strong at all.

Picking up the flyers, I opened the shop door before I had time to think about it. The heat hit me like a punch in the face. I held onto the doorframe, swaying, before inching my foot towards the pavement. As it touched the ground, Jeremy Eyelashes jogged around the corner.

Of all the people.

Jeremy was the exact opposite of me. Super-popular.

Super-sporty. And, according to the girls, super-fit. Yasmin, the most popular girl in our year, had called him Jeremy Eyelashes a few years ago, and it had stuck.

'Hi, Pete. Are you better?' He kept running on the spot while he was talking, his trainers almost blinding me with their dazzling whiteness.

'I'm ... um ... ah ... I'm fine. One hundred per cent fine, actually.'

He gave me a funny look and jogged off.

I closed my eyes, cringing. *One hundred per cent fine?* No doubt he'd tell everyone and they'd think I was even more of a weirdo than they did already. I suddenly remembered the flyers in my hand. I groaned. I hadn't even given him a flyer. I stepped back inside – I couldn't face going out after that.

Dad rushed out of the kitchen and pulled me into a hug. 'You did it!'

I wriggled out of his hold. 'Hardly, Dad. I put one foot outside.'

He pulled a pen out of his apron pocket with a flourish, like a magician pulling a rabbit out of a hat. 'It still counts. Tick the chart at once!'

*

At eleven o'clock – opening time – the dough was ready and the oven was hot. Dad sprayed polish on the counter and wiped it for the billionth time. The shop had never looked so gleaming.

Anna, true to her word, had rushed back from band practice and was running down the high street handing out flyers by herself. So where was everybody? I looked right and left out of the window. It was eerily quiet – like the aftermath of a zombie apocalypse.

I sighed. 'There's no way we'll make enough money at this rate.'

Dad squeezed my shoulder. 'Let's wash up while we're waiting.'

I followed him into the kitchen, feeling as wrung out as the old tea towel I picked up to dry the dishes. All our hard work for nothing. If only our pizza shop was in a better spot. Fox Pizza had hungry shoppers walking past it all day, and I bet they had robots to do their washing up.

Anna suddenly appeared in the doorway with Useless. She was chewing her sleeve. 'Do you want the good news or the bad news?'

'Good news,' Dad and I said together.

'We've got our first customer.'

'And the bad news?' I asked.

There was a short silence. 'You'd better come and see for yourself.'

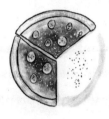

Chapter Thirteen

Archie Boyle was leaning on the counter in his shiny, red football shirt, with a flyer in his hand. Zach was on his phone outside, looking up at our new sign.

'What's this about magical pizzas?' said Archie, waving the flyer about. 'You gonna turn me into Harry Potter or something? Sounds about right, weirdo.'

Anna leant over the counter towards him. 'That weirdo has more goodness in his little toe than you have in your whole body.' She pushed him in the chest.

'Woah!' Archie stumbled backwards and fell to the floor, mouth gaping like a goldfish.

'You're not meant to attack the customers,' I hissed, as he scrambled to his feet.

Anna looked from me to Archie and back. 'You're not seriously going to serve him?'

'We need all the money we can get,' I said, under my breath.

Archie was looking up at the menu. 'Twenty pounds for a *slice* of pizza? Are you having a laugh? I want a free one, for being assaulted.'

I shook my head. 'I can't do that.'

He leant towards me and whispered, 'Free pizza. Or else.'

My skin crawled. I didn't want to know what 'else' was. 'OK, but hurry up.'

He frowned at the menu. 'I don't get it. What's Paws 'n' Pizza?'

'It turns you into your spirit animal,' said Anna. 'I changed into a fox, which stands for mischief and playfulness.'

'Yeah right.'

I nodded. 'It's true.' I pointed to the Animal potion on the shelf. 'We sprinkle a drop of this onto a slice of margherita, and in a couple of minutes you'll turn into an animal.'

He peered at the potion. 'What is it?'

'Secret recipe,' I replied.

He turned to leave. 'Whatever.'

'Send Zach in,' said Anna. 'He can tell you all about it.'

Archie stopped, looked at Zach through the window then came back to the counter. 'What did you turn into, Pete? No, let me guess.' He rubbed his chin then gave a nasty grin. 'A worm. Lives in the mud, hardly ever seen, but when it pops up you wish it'd go back down, 'cos it's ugly as hell.'

I cleared my throat and looked down. 'A butterfly.'

He sniggered. 'What does that stand for? Girly and pathetic?'

'It means he's about to go through a big change in his life,' said Anna.

I glanced at her. 'Really?'

'According to Google.' She raised an eyebrow at Archie. 'I reckon you'd be a lion, or an eagle. Something strong and brave.'

He puffed his chest out. 'Fine. I'm starving, so hurry up.'

'Ready for our first pizza, Dad,' I yelled. 'Take a seat, Archie. It'll be a few minutes.'

But he didn't sit down. He just stood there, staring at me. Dad brought the pizza through and I put it in the oven. When it was ready, I cut it up and measured a drop of Animal potion onto a slice.

Archie watched me with suspicion as he stuffed it into his mouth. 'What a surprise. I'm still *human*,' he said, once he'd finished chewing. 'I want my money back.'

'Er . . . you didn't pay for it.'

'Don't care.' He put his hand out. 'Twenty pounds.' He looked down at his football shirt, eyes widening. The material was tightening around his chest, the muscles bulging beneath it. 'No way . . . this is . . . wahhh!' His clothes started to rip apart at the seams, revealing his skin, which was tough, hairy and . . . pink. 'What the—?' He held up his hands and stared at them, as his fingers fused into trotters. Then he lost his balance and landed on all fours, facing Zach, on the other side of the window.

'He's a PIG!' screamed Zach, his eyeballs almost popping out of his skull.

Archie lumbered around to face us. He had a flat, pink snout and huge ears, and his clothes were strewn around the shop floor. He stamped his little trotter and let out a high-pitched squeal.

I bit my lip to stop myself laughing. 'Don't worry. It'll wear off soon.'

He squealed again and started running around the shop, as fast as his trotters could take him. We leapt behind the counter to get out of his way.

Zach stopped a woman with an enormous buggy who was walking past, and pointed through the window. 'Check this out!'

'What?' she said, peering through the glass. 'Hold on. What's a pig doing in a . . .' She stepped back to look at the sign. 'What *is* this place?'

Zach turned and shouted towards the high street. 'Hey everybody, you've got to see this!'

Mr Campbell from number seventy-four stopped to look, then a group of teenagers. Soon there was a big crowd outside the window, everyone holding their phones over each other's heads to get a good shot of the pig in the pizza shop.

Zach had his phone pressed to the window. 'You've put on a bit of weight, Arch. Don't hog all the pizza.' He turned to the woman with the buggy. 'Do you get it? Don't *hog* all the pizza?'

Suddenly Archie froze. He lifted his tail and a revolting stench filled the air.

'He's done a poo!' yelled Zach, doubled over with laughter. He shouted back over the crowd. 'Did you see that? He's done a *poo!*'

The crowd erupted.

Archie ran around the counter, leaving behind a steaming pile of ploppy pig poo. I was about to re-assure him it would be over any minute, when his whole body quivered from snout to tail. Within seconds he'd changed back to his normal self.

I passed him his clothes and he pulled on his shorts. Then he stood up and walked around the counter, trying to pull on his shirt, but it got tangled around his neck. He fought with it, getting angrier by the second, before stepping backwards, straight into the pile of poo. He looked down at his squelchy brown foot, then up at me, eyes hot with fury.

'I'll get you back for this.' Picking up his trainers, he limped out of the shop, then went straight up to Zach and very slowly and purposefully wiped his stinky foot on the leg of Zach's tracky bottoms.

'What you doing, mate?' laughed Zach.

'I am not your *mate*. I will never be your *mate* again,' said Archie, pushing Zach out of the way. The crowd moved apart, holding their noses, to let him through.

'Where's your sense of humour?' shouted Zach after him, tapping his phone. 'There. Sent to all. I'm sure they'll see the funny side.'

Zach's video spread the word far wider than we could ever have done with a handful of flyers. It was the best publicity we could have asked for. But I felt really bad about Archie. I remembered how embarrassed I was when I had the panic attack, with everyone watching. It was *awful*.

I sent him a message to ask if he was OK, but he didn't reply, and soon we were so busy I forgot about him. We had a queue of customers outside the shop, desperate to try our pizzas. A queue! I couldn't remember the last time we'd had *anyone* waiting, let alone a queue.

The woman with the buggy wanted her triplets to try the Mozzarella-la-la-la. She took their dummies out and gave them each a small slice of pizza to chew on. Only seconds later, they were warbling 'Twinkle Twinkle Little Star' in harmony, in the sweetest baby voices.

It gave me goosebumps. I glanced at Anna and Dad, who'd come out of the kitchen to watch. They were both as spellbound as I was. When the potion wore off, the mother asked for another slice, but I pointed to the queue and explained she had to go to the back.

Mr Campbell was very confused. He didn't under-stand why he couldn't have his usual – a Hawaiian with mushrooms. Once I'd explained the new menu to him, he said his only regret was never being able to do a cartwheel, so I gave him a slice of Pizza the Action. He put his hands in the air and cartwheeled around the shop, then staggered out, green but happy.

The group of teenagers all chose Pizza Pan. We let them in one by one, and ducked as each of them swooped around the shop. They enjoyed it so much that they all rushed to the back of the queue.

Halfway through the morning, I'd popped into the kitchen to get more plates when I heard a voice I recognised. Jeremy Eyelashes. My heart jumped. The most popular boy in the year was in *my* pizza shop!

I ran out of the kitchen, skidding to a halt by the counter. 'You're here!' Even as I said it, I winced.

But he just grinned, his eyes wide with wonder as he read the menu. 'This looks . . . different. Can I take a photo?'

'Sure.' I stood up straight and put on my best smile.

He pointed up. 'Of the menu?'

I rubbed the back of my neck. 'Of course, I knew that.' I could tell Anna was shaking her head in despair without even looking at her.

'There,' said Jeremy, tapping his phone. 'I've sent it to all my contacts.'

'How many have you got?' I asked.

'About five hundred?'

I blinked at him. I could count mine on two hands.

'Jeremy!' called a voice outside. 'Yoohoo! Future husband!'

Yasmin had barged to the front of the queue and was waving her phone at Jeremy through the window.

He turned his back to her and rolled his eyes. I giggled nervously, pretending I had girls throwing themselves at me all the time.

'Any bright ideas of how to get rid of her?' asked Jeremy.

'I do, actually. It won't get rid of her, but it'll help you escape.' I turned to the potion shelf. 'Where's the Shrink?'

Jeremy laughed. 'I was joking.' He peered at the potions. 'But now I'm kind of intrigued.'

'Dad?' I called. 'Have you got the Shrink potion?'

'No,' he replied.

'That's odd. How about this one?' I picked the

Invisibility potion off the shelf and showed it to Jeremy. 'It'll do the same job.'

As soon as Jeremy bit into the pizza, his eyes lit up. 'This is epic!'

'It's the same recipe as before,' I said. 'Just with a little extra something on top.'

He closed his eyes, savouring every mouthful. 'I guess I haven't been here for a while.'

Two minutes later, Yasmin was peering through

the window. 'Where's he gone?' She looked down at her phone. 'It says he's still here on *Find my Boyfriends*.'

'I knew it. She's tracking me!' hissed Jeremy's voice, floating in front of us. The Invisibility potion had worked its magic. 'How long have I got?'

'About three minutes before it wears off,' I said.

'I'll be back soon. This place is awesome. Everyone's going to love it.'

'Bye, Jeremy. See you—' But before I could finish, the door swung open by itself and he was gone.

'What the—?' Yasmin's eyes opened wide as her phone was snatched out of her hand by what appeared to be nothing more than thin air. She tried to grab it but it kept floating out of her reach. She looked left and right. 'Is this a prank? Is someone filming me? You can't post it without my permission.'

Her phone eventually landed back in her hand. She tapped it. 'Why can't I see Jeremy's location anymore?' She marched into the shop, straight through to the kitchen, then back to the counter. 'Where'd he go? Is he hiding somewhere?'

I felt a bit sorry for her. She seemed genuinely upset. 'Don't worry about him, Yasmin.' I pointed at the menu. 'Would you like to try one of our new pizzas?'

She studied me closely. 'You know my name?'

I cleared my throat. 'We're in the same English set.'

'Really?'

'Yup. I haven't been at school for a while.'

She stared at me like I was an alien species. 'I've never heard you speak.'

'I guess I'm one of the quiet ones.'

Anna snorted. 'I beg to differ.'

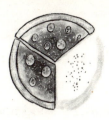

Chapter Fourteen

The afternoon was even busier.

Thanks to Jeremy's contact list, the queue was full of all the cool kids from school – the sporty ones, the popular ones, the older ones. They loved our magical pizzas, especially Pizza the Action, Pizza Pan and Where the Olive are You? A few brave people tried Paws 'n' Pizza, once I'd warned them they couldn't choose what they were going to turn into. There were no more pigs, but throughout the day we had a polar bear, an eagle, two jaguars, three rabbits, a dragonfly and a wolf in the shop, luckily not at the same time.

I felt my shoulders drop as the day went on. I'd been so worried about seeing everyone from school, but most of them were really friendly. Some people asked if I was going back to school next term. I just smiled and said, 'I'm not sure,' but inside I was thinking *maybe it wouldn't be too bad after all?*

At some point during the afternoon, Useless snuck into the front of the shop and curled up by the window. Dad didn't say anything. Maybe he was too busy to notice. But the customers loved it. Some of them crouched down and tickled her tummy while they were waiting for their pizza.

At closing time there was still a huge queue. Most of the children had gone to bed, but there were plenty of grown-ups keen to try our magical pizzas. We decided to keep the shop open, although Anna had to go home.

Mr Shah turned up after midnight, with huge, dark bags under his eyes. He said he didn't have any food in the house and he was struggling to finish his marking from the end of term. He only lived down the road, so I told him to go and get his schoolbooks. By the time he got back, there was a bubbling hot slice of The Need for Speed waiting for him. He wolfed it down and finished the marking in under two minutes. When Dad thrust a glass of red wine into his hand and said he was welcome any time, his eyes welled up.

When he'd left, I locked the door and collapsed on a stool with my head on the counter.

'Holy macaroni!' Dad looked up from the till. 'We've sold three hundred and five slices of pizza today!'

I felt my cheeks reddening with excitement as I did the maths in my head. 'That means we only need to sell one hundred and eighty slices tomorrow!'

Dad beamed at me, his eyes properly twinkling for the first time in ages. 'Come here, my clever boy.' He put his arms out and gave me an enormous hug.

I grinned up at him. I couldn't believe it. My plan to save our home had worked.

But the next day, it all went wrong. And when I say wrong, I mean utterly disastrously wrong. And when I say utterly disastrously wrong, I mean . . .

You get the idea.

I woke up feeling like Dak when he steps into his snowspeeder in *The Empire Strikes Back*.

Right now, I feel like I could take on the whole Empire myself.

I was buzzing to get downstairs, put my apron on and start serving. There were already a few keen customers waiting outside the shop – I'd seen them through a crack in my bedroom curtain.

It started off well. Jeremy was our first customer. He'd been waiting for *two* hours. He had a Muscles and Mozzarella and managed to pick all of us up – me, Anna, Useless *and* Dad – using just one hand.

Our next customer was a girl with a long wonky plait called Prisha Singh. She spent ages cuddling Useless before revealing it was her birthday, so we sang 'Happy Birthday' and offered her a free slice of pizza. She chose Pizza Pan and spent the next couple of minutes happily flying around the shop. She said it was the best birthday treat ever and leant over the counter to give me a kiss on the cheek before she left, which was awkward.

Then Lisa Petch came in. Lisa was a quiet, serious girl in my maths set. I told her what all the pizzas did, and she eventually settled on a slice of Smarto Tomato.

'How will I know if it's working?' she asked, once she'd chewed the last mouthful.

I sat down opposite her at the table. 'You'll know.'

Her whole body suddenly twitched. 'I feel,' her eyes widened, 'electric!'

'It's working. Let's see how clever you are.'

I searched on my phone for a calculation, while Lisa giggled and bounced up and down in her chair. That's when I should have realised something was up. I'd never seen her laugh before.

'Try this one.' I showed her the screen. 'It's calculus.'

$$\log_4(x-4y25\sqrt{z})\log_4(x-4y2z5)$$

Lisa hooted with laughter and clapped her hands. 'I need a pen and paper, quickly.'

'Who knew maths was so hilarious,' said Anna, as

she got the pencil and notebook from next to the till.

Lisa scribbled something down and showed it to me, then clapped a hand over her mouth, like she was trying to stop her giggles from bubbling out.

Anna leant over my shoulder and read what Lisa had written out loud. *'How many tickles does it take to get an octopus to laugh?'*

'Ten!' Lisa yelled, bouncing up and down, even higher than before. 'Do you get it? Ten tickles?'

I shot a glance at Anna. 'I get it, but it's not calculus.'

'It's not calculus!' repeated Lisa, doubling over and grabbing her sides. 'You're so funny!'

Anna looked from me to Lisa. 'He's really not.'

'I've got another one!' said Lisa. 'Why do you never see elephants hiding up in trees?'

I frowned. 'I don't know. Why do you never see elephants hiding up in trees?'

'Because they're really good at it!' Her face creased up again as she howled with laughter.

Anna turned to me. 'You must have given her the Laughter potion by mistake.'

That really set Lisa off. She grabbed Anna's arm, tears streaming down her cheeks.

I shook my head. 'I'm sure I gave her Intelligence. Dad, can you come here?'

He came out of the kitchen, wiping the back of his floury hand on his bandana. 'Sounds like someone's enjoying their Cheesy Chuckles, eh?'

'She didn't have a Cheesy Chuckles,' I said, as Lisa collapsed into another fit of giggles. 'She had a Smarto Tomato.'

She launched into a new joke. 'What kind of exercise do lazy people do?'

'I don't know,' said Dad. 'What kind of exercise *do* lazy people do?'

Her face suddenly dropped. 'I don't know,' she said glumly.

'It's worn off,' I said. 'Whatever it was.'

The next customer was Lisa's mum. She asked for Pizza the Action and spent the next few minutes backflipping around the shop. I started questioning myself. Perhaps I *had* given Lisa the Laughter potion by mistake?

That's when Ben walked in. He was the shortest boy in our year, not much taller than the counter.

'Leaning Tower of Pizza, please!' he said.

But it didn't make him grow. Well, not how we expected.

'What the . . . ?' Ben turned his hands over. 'Why are my palms hairy?'

Anna leant towards me and whispered, 'It looks like you gave him the Animal potion.'

I picked up the Grow potion from the counter next to the till, where I'd left it. 'I definitely used this one. You saw me!'

Within a minute, every inch of Ben's skin was covered in thick, dark fur. 'What's happening to me?' he wailed.

I tried to smile reassuringly. 'I'd do anything to look like Chewbacca.'

'Who?' asked Ben.

'The hairy guy in *Star Wars*,' said Anna.

I was about to explain that Chewbacca was in fact a legendary Wookiee warrior, when Dad came out. He took one look at Ben and beckoned me into the kitchen. 'This can't go on.'

Chapter Fifteen

There was uproar when Dad popped his head outside to tell everyone we were closing.

'I've been queueing for ages!'

'We've driven two hours to get here!'

'WE WANT MAGICAL PIZZAS!'

I was furious too. 'What are you doing, Dad? This is our last day to make money. We're going to be evicted tomorrow if we don't sell enough pizzas.'

'We can't serve customers if the potions aren't working properly. I've got my reputation to think about,' Dad replied.

I blinked, my face reddening. 'So let's test them again. We know Strength, Flight and Agility are fine, so we can leave them. Grow and Intelligence don't work, so we don't need to do them either.'

'And the Shrink potion's disappeared,' said Anna. 'So we can't do that one.'

I counted on my fingers. 'That leaves seven potions. It won't take long if we test them at the same time.'

Dad slowly nodded. 'OK.'

I closed the blinds, trying to ignore the angry faces pressed to the other side of the window. We tested the Invisibility, Animal and Turbo potions first. They were all fine. Then we tested Replication by making more Flight potion. It worked perfectly. I felt my shoulders drop. We only had three more to test. We'd be back open in no time!

'I'll test Laughter,' I said.

'I'll do Voice,' said Anna.

'And I'll do Shapeshifter,' said Dad.

A few minutes later, I felt the familiar fizzing sensation running up and down my spine, like I'd shoved my fingers into an electrical socket. We watched each other, nervously. It was one thing waiting when you knew what was going to happen to you, quite another when you didn't.

'Feeling funny?' Anna asked, looking at me.

'No.'

'That's strange, because there's something very funny on your shoulder.'

I looked down and nearly jumped out of my skin. Three little fingers were sticking out of my right T-shirt sleeve. 'Arrghhh! Get them off me!'

Anna reached forward to tug them. 'It's like they're attached to you.'

'Let me have a go.' Dad gave them a proper yank.

'Ouch!' Lifting my sleeve, I saw a tiny hand emerging from my shoulder. 'They *are* attached to me!' We watched in horror as the tiny hand grew bigger and bigger.

'Make it stop!' I shrieked, slapping the fingers with my left hand.

Dad and Anna looked on, helpless, as a wrist emerged from my shoulder, followed by a forearm and an upper arm.

Useless wouldn't stop barking at me, so Dad put her in the garden.

Anna scratched her cheek. 'You've got a *whole new arm*.'

We all peered at my new hand as I held it up in front of my face. I'd never seen such clean fingernails before. I was freaked out, but also weirdly excited. 'This would be so useful for gaming!'

'Or making pizza,' said Dad.

'Or scratching,' said Anna, rubbing her neck. 'Can you scratch my back for me? I feel like I'm covered in mosquito bites.'

I peered at her face. 'It looks more like . . . scales.'

'Scales?'

I looked closer. 'Brown scales. Like Tony.'

'Who?' she asked.

'Tony the goldfish. Do you remember Tony? He went all brown and manky just before he died.'

'Great.'

'Holy guacamole!' shouted Dad. I turned around to see him hovering a few centimetres off the floor and rising rapidly, like a helium balloon.

'I've got you!' I stretched my three arms up to grab him, but he was out of reach. He kept on floating upwards, and within seconds he was stuck to the ceiling, like a butterfly trapped with a pin.

'Help!' he yelled.

'I can't feel my legs!' Anna's skin was now covered in dark brown scales. She collapsed onto her knees then fell forwards until she was writhing around on her tummy, her legs stuck together. Her glasses fell off, so I put them on the counter to keep them safe.

'What happens when it wears off?' said Dad. 'I'll fall like a ton of bricks!'

'What about me?' shrieked Anna, as her arms fused into her body. 'I'm turning into a manky goldfish! How am I going to breathe without water?'

My head was spinning but I knew I had to stay calm. 'Anna, I'll run the bath and get you into it.'

'How?' she wailed.

'I'll drag you up the stairs if I have to.' I looked up. 'Dad, you need to wriggle across the ceiling, then climb down the wall.'

'Who do you think I am? Spiderman?'

'Fair point.' I dragged the table under Dad. At least he wouldn't have so far to fall when the potion wore off. Then I ran upstairs and turned on the bath taps. My head was pounding. *What had happened to the potions?*

I felt something tickling my left shoulder, and looked down to see another tiny hand, this time sticking out of my left sleeve. It grew and grew, until it was the same length as the other three. I groaned. Three arms was helpful, four arms was ridiculous.

Suddenly Dad screamed. I'd never heard Dad scream before, so I knew it was bad.

I didn't realise how bad until I was halfway down the stairs.

A huge, dark brown snake stared back at me with beady, black eyes, its head and neck raised off the ground. And when I say huge, I mean GIGANTIC. Its head was the size and shape of a small coffin; its tail so long, it filled the front of the shop, its fat coils pushing up against the window blinds.

I prickled with fear, like all the skin wanted to crawl off my body. Anna had turned into a *giant snake*! Where was Tony the goldfish when I needed him? My first instinct was to run back upstairs and dive under the duvet. But then I saw Dad, stuck to the ceiling, with an expression of pure fear on his face. He was shaking so hard, I worried he might fall off into the snake's coils.

I took a deep breath, trying to slow my heart, which felt like it was being attacked by a hundred tiny drummers. Now would *not* be a good time to have another panic attack. I forced a smile out. 'It's OK, Dad. It's just Anna.'

She slid towards me on the staircase, until her head was at the same level as mine. I pressed my back into the wall and laughed nervously. 'H-h-hi, Anna . . . You're not going to . . . um . . . bite us or squeeze us to death or anything, are you?'

She returned my gaze. I *felt* her telling me how sick it was to be a snake and of course she wasn't going to

hurt us. She didn't actually say the words, because . . .
well . . . snakes can't talk.

'Just stay away from Dad,' I whispered. 'You know
how he is about snakes.'

I could have sworn she winked at me. My shoulders
dropped, just a tiny bit. 'You can relax, Dad. She's not
going to bite.'

'How can I relax when I'm stuck to the ceiling?' he
muttered.

I reached out with one of my five hands (they were
still coming) to see what Anna's scales felt like, when
there was a loud banging on the window.

'Pete!' The voice was unmistakable. It was Archie
Boyle. 'Pete!'

Anna-the-snake reared back and her mouth gaped
open revealing an inky blackness and two fangs as
long as scythes. She darted her head towards the
window, hissing.

Black mouth. I had a flashback to my Year Two
Africa project. Brown scales, coffin-shaped head,
black mouth . . .

'Dad?' I whispered. 'She's a black mamba!'

'Is that bad?'

I was about to tell him that one bite could kill fifteen grown men, but I didn't think that would help, so I kept quiet.

Another knock on the window. 'I know you're there, Pete. Let me in!'

Anna jerked her head towards the noise.

'Tell him to shut up!' whispered Dad. 'He's scaring her.'

I crept downstairs and opened the door an inch. Archie pushed his face into the gap, his eyes wild. A woman I vaguely recognised was behind him, trying to peer into the shop. 'We need to talk,' he said. 'I've messed up.' He squinted at my shoulder. 'Are those . . . fingers?'

I grabbed him by his football top and pulled him inside, then quickly closed the door behind him.

Anna let out an almighty hiss. Her black tongue, the length of a broom, flicked out towards him.

He opened his mouth to scream but I clamped one of my five – no six – hands over it. 'It's Anna.' I dropped my hand. 'The snake is Anna.'

Eyes wide as moons, Archie took in my extra arms and Dad clinging to the ceiling. 'I . . . I didn't mean to—'

'*What* have you done?'

'You know your . . . um . . .' He pointed at the potion bottles on the shelf.

'Pizza toppings?' I said.

'Yeah, those. I mixed a few of—'

But he didn't finish the sentence, because Anna-the-snake lunged at him, her mouth wide open, fangs dripping with venom.

Chapter Sixteen

Without thinking, I jumped in front of Archie. Anna recoiled just in time, her fangs missing my face by a whisker.

Dad gasped.

I could feel Archie's heart pounding against my back and smell the sharp stench of his sweat.

'You saved my life,' he panted, over my shoulder.

Anna was watching him warily, mouth still wide open.

I let out a huge breath. 'She wouldn't have bitten you. At least, I don't think she would.'

'You saved my life, mate. You saved my *life*.'

I twisted around to look at him. 'How did you get in last night? I remember locking the door.'

He put a trembling hand in his pocket and pulled out a bottle. The Shrink potion.

Anna hissed.

'That's where it was!' I said.

'I nicked it yesterday,' said Archie, 'when you were putting my pizza in the oven. I dunno why, I wasn't going to do anything with it. Not until I was completely humiliated in front of tons of people. Do you know how that feels?'

'I do, actually.'

He looked blank.

'The swimming pool?' I muttered.

He frowned. 'What swimming pool?'

I looked at him quizzically. I'd assumed my panic attack on the diving board was seared onto everyone's minds – that the whole school was still gossiping about it. But it looked like Archie couldn't even remember it.

He shrugged. 'Anyway . . . I set my alarm for three o'clock this morning and used some of this shrink stuff to squeeze under the door.'

'How much did you take?' I asked, peering under the door, at the slimmest of cracks.

'A big gulp . . . and suddenly the door's the size of a mountain and the gap's a dark tunnel, full of giant cobwebs, and then I'm in here. I'm panicking 'cos I think I'm never going to grow, then I shoot back up and I'm tall again.'

'Then what?' I asked.

'I started this end,' he said, pointing at the row of potions next to the till. 'I tipped some of this one – *Intelligence* – into this one, *Laughter*. Then I moved along to the next one, mixing them together. I just wanted to get you back, cause a bit of drama. But this morning, Mum asked me to come and get a pizza with her. She wanted to know what all the fuss was about.'

I looked towards the door. Of course, that's who it was. His mum.

'I panicked. What if I'd made them dangerous, mixing them up? I don't want Mum to die. Know what I mean?'

I caught Dad's eye. 'I do.'

Suddenly Archie gasped and pointed at Anna-the-snake. Four limbs were splitting away from her long shiny body, and brown messy hair was sprouting from her scaly head.

'She's changing back!' I cried.

'So are you!' said Archie.

I looked down. My extra arms were shrinking. I was becoming less octopus by the second.

'WAH!' shouted Dad, falling like a sack of rocks. He landed on the table, eyes closed.

'Dad!' I ran to his side, heart racing.

'Noooo!' cried Anna, running to his other side. She was human again, apart from a few brown scales on her cheeks.

'Is he . . . is he . . . ?' Archie was frozen to the spot, wringing his hands.

'Well padded?' Dad opened his eyes and winked. 'Yes, he is.'

I threw myself at him, breathing a deep sigh of relief. Finally, the potions had worn off. Dad and Anna were safe. We had enough working potions to open the shop, and if we were quick about it, we could still reach our ten thousand pound target in time.

Something wet landed on the back of my head. I stood up. A large drop of water fell on Dad's cheek. Then another.

'Why's it raining?' asked Anna, putting her glasses back on.

We all looked up. Water was dripping off the ceiling. A *lot* of water.

A chunk of plaster fell onto the table, narrowly missing Dad's legs. Something groaned above our heads. Something loud and metallic and ominous.

'Quick! Everyone, move back!' I shouted. Anna and I dragged Dad off the table just in time, as half the ceiling collapsed.

A torrent of water flooded into the shop.

A huge cloud of plaster and dust.

An almighty crash as something enormous plummeted to the ground, smashing the table to pieces.

My mouth hung open. *What on earth?*

As the dust cleared, the blood drained from my face.

There, in a pile of rubble and plaster, was our bath.

We surveyed the wreckage. Bits of plaster rained down from the ceiling. We could see straight through the gaping hole into the bathroom above. Water was gushing out of broken pipes, spraying everything.

Anna took her glasses off and wiped them with her cardigan. 'Which potion did *that*?'

I swallowed. 'It wasn't a potion. It was me. I left the taps on.'

'Archie!' shrieked a voice outside. 'What was that? Are you OK?'

'I'm fine, Mum,' he called, pulling a blob of wet plaster out of his hair.

Dad looked at him. 'You should go.'

He shook his head firmly. 'I'll help you clear up this mess.'

'Don't you think you've done enough?' Anna wheeled around to face him, eyes blazing. 'This is all your fault! I should have dug my fangs into you while I had the chance. You little—'

'Leave it, Anna.' I turned to Archie. 'You should go home.'

He looked down at his feet. 'I didn't mean to . . .'

'I know.' I opened the door just wide enough to let him through.

Halfway out, he turned to look at me. 'Let me know if there's anything I can do.' He blinked. 'Anything.'

'Are you open?' called Archie's mum, through the gap.

'No. Closed.' I quickly shut the door, ignoring the shouts from the crowd. 'Closed for good.' My eyes filled with tears. 'I'm sorry, Dad.'

He squeezed my shoulder. 'It's not your fault, love. The joists have been eaten to bits by worms. It's a miracle it didn't happen earlier, to be honest.'

Tears of frustration ran down my cheeks. 'It's not just the bath. It's everything. I ruined *everything*.' With no warning, great creaking sobs rose up in my chest. Dad put his arm around me and Anna took my hand.

Once I started crying, I couldn't stop. I cried and cried until I felt hollow, like I was the one with the hole in me, not the ceiling.

Dad passed me a tissue and I noisily blew my nose, then looked up at Anna. 'You were right. I should have gone out with flyers in the first place. Rather than coming up with a ridiculous idea . . . I mean, magical pizzas, what was I thinking?'

'It was a *great* idea!' cried Anna.

I snorted. 'It failed, big time. Look at this place.' I gazed at the bath and the debris surrounding it. 'I was meant to save our home. Not trash it.'

The spray suddenly changed direction, pointing straight towards us. Our hair and clothes were instantly soaked, plastered to our bodies. I wiped my eyes. 'You've got to be kidding.'

Dad put his arms around us and led us to the staircase, the only dry place in the whole shop. 'Don't move. I'm going to turn off the stop cock.' He carefully climbed over the piles of rubble to get to the kitchen.

I sat down on the stairs, my head in my hands.

Anna sat down next to me. 'What happens now?'

I looked up and sighed. 'We failed to make ten

thousand pounds, so we'll be evicted tomorrow.'
I sniffed. 'Dad said something about moving into
Craig's pub until we find somewhere else.'

Anna glanced at the bath and nudged me. 'Maybe
it's not a bad thing. Not sure what you ever saw in
this place, to be honest.'

I smiled. 'It *is* a bit of a dump.'

'Water's off,' shouted Dad.

We watched the spray of water lose power, until
it gradually stopped. Anna looked at me and made a
face. 'Your nose is covered in snot.'

I tried to look at my nose, which made me
cross-eyed.

Anna giggled. 'Will you get another shop?'

'Only if the bank lends us more money.' I glanced
at the hole in the ceiling. 'Seems unlikely.'

'What are you going to do with the potions? You've
still got . . .' she counted on her fingers, 'Strength,
Animal, Replication, Flight, Invisibility, Turbo, Agility
and Shrink. Eight potions that work.'

I bit my lip. 'I think it's time we returned them to
Silva Tregoning.'

Chapter Seventeen

We stood in the middle of my bedroom and looked around. Dad smiled at me. 'One step at a time, eh? Let's start with your clothes.'

He whistled as we packed. I knew he was trying to keep my spirits up, but I felt increasingly miserable. I'd slept in this bedroom every night since I was born. Everything I packed away held a memory. But I was even sadder about the things I couldn't take. Like my cosy reading corner, warm from the pizza oven below. Like the *Star Wars* stickers on the wall, next to my bed. Like the grumpy face Anna drew behind the curtain when Dad told us off for eating all the pepperoni.

My bedroom was part of me, as much as my hair was part of me, and the thought of being ripped apart from it was unthinkable. Let alone the thought of going outside. I was trying my hardest to push that to the back of my mind.

One step at a time.

We moved onto my Lego, putting the broken pieces of the Star Destroyer into a box. It had been such a crazy week, I hadn't had a second to rebuild it. Dad was about to tape the box up when I grabbed his arm. 'Wait. We're missing the crew member.'

He frowned. 'Which one's that?'

'The one with a grey cap and a headset.'

'I'm sure he'll turn up. He can go in another box.'

I shook my head. 'He needs to go in here with the Star Destroyer. It's his home.'

Dad looked like he was going to say something, then changed his mind. He bent down to look under the bed. 'He's got to be here somewhere.' But I knew he was stressing about time, so I told him not to worry and taped up the box, blinking back tears.

That night, exhausted but unable to sleep, I listened to Dad packing up next door. I played with the edge of a TARDIS sticker that was peeling off the wall. I wouldn't mind leaving home if we had a TARDIS. A home from home. It could whisk us off to a different time, a different place, maybe even a different planet, where we'd battle evil aliens and have all sorts of adventures.

It was midnight when I heard a strange sound coming from Dad's bedroom. I peeked through the crack in his door. He was sitting on the bed holding a yellow dress, tears running down his cheeks. Dad was crying? I'd never seen him cry before. I didn't realise dads *could* cry. It felt like a knife going through my heart.

I peered closer. I knew that dress. It was the one Mum was wearing in the photo of me and her on the stairs. I was a tiny baby and she was holding me in her arms, smiling down at me. We were on a beach in the Outer Hebrides, miles of white sand stretching away behind us. I coughed and went in.

Dad dropped the dress on his lap and quickly wiped his face. 'Can't sleep?' I shook my head and he patted the bed. 'Hop in.'

He leant over to pick up a roll of bubble wrap as I snuggled under the duvet, then he carefully wrapped all the photos on his bedside table: him and Mum on the edge of a mountain, carrying backpacks; Mum leaning on a surfboard, grinning at the camera; the two of them sitting on the back of an elephant.

I kicked Dad's bottom, through the duvet. 'You did some fun stuff together, you and Mum.'

He smiled, holding a photo of her on a bike, in front of a huge red bridge. 'She was full of life, your mum. Always planning the next adventure.'

I bit my lip. I'd never really thought about it before. Mum and Dad had a life before I was born. And not just any old life. I thought about Mum's stuff in the attic . . . my old camel wall-hanging . . . the fridge magnets from places I'd never even heard of. They'd had an *exciting* life, travelling all over the world. Then they'd bought the shop, Mum had died and Dad had been forced to churn out pizza after pizza, day after day, to pay the bank back. It must have felt like a noose around his neck. He'd become a prisoner in his own house. As trapped as I was. And now we were going to move, and it would start all over again. We'd owe the bank more money, we'd be trapped in another house.

Unless . . .

A shiver ran down my spine. I'd had an idea. A

bonkers idea, but I didn't seem capable of any other sort. I cleared my throat and slipped out of Dad's bed. 'Sleep well, Dad. Love you.'

He put the bubble wrap down and ruffled my hair. 'You know you're my favourite child, right?'

I laughed. 'I'm your *only* child, Dad.' Back in my room, I picked up my phone and sent a message. As I was putting it down, I noticed something shiny under the radiator on the other side of the room.

The crew member.

'There you are!' I got out of bed, picked him up and carefully blew the dust away. I found the box with the Star Destroyer and nestled the minifigure down amongst the broken chunks of Lego. 'I'll build you a new home soon, I promise,' I whispered, before closing the box.

'Morning!' Dad poked his head through my door. 'Craig's downstairs. We're taking the last boxes over to his. Will you be OK?' He looked around my bedroom. 'There's not much to do on your own.'

I yawned and picked up my phone, waving it in the air. 'Never alone with a phone.'

He stopped halfway out the door. 'Don't go near the bathroom.'

'Use the bucket in the garden, I know.'

As he closed the door, I quickly swung my legs out of bed. I'd had an awful realisation. Dad must have packed Luke Skywalker and Han Solo away. I had no idea where, and I didn't have time to look through all the boxes.

I'd have to do this on my own.

My heart was pounding against my ribcage as I opened the shop door, like it was desperate to get out. It was twenty-nine days since I'd left the house. Almost a month.

I squeezed my eyes shut. *Remember what Dr Shannon said. If you have another panic attack, sit somewhere calm, slow your breathing, and don't forget – it will end soon.*

I opened my eyes and kept them fixed on my trainers as I stepped onto the pavement and locked the door behind me. I took a deep breath. The air was hot and smelled different. Like I'd just stepped off a plane in a foreign country. I took a few wobbly steps, then looked up. I was still outside the shop. At this rate, it was going to take me all day to get to the end of the road. I started to panic. I couldn't do it. I was a flailing jellyfish, in a very fast current.

Suddenly a firm hand gripped my arm. 'Wherever you're going, I'm going too, butthead.'

I looked up into Anna's grinning face, a wave of relief crashing over me. She didn't even question my plan, and soon she was dragging me down the pavement. I clung to her arm like a drowning man to a lifebuoy. Useless trotted along on her other side.

We stopped at the postbox on the corner of Harwood Road and the high street.

'You OK?' she asked.

I wiped my hands on my jeans. *Was* I OK? The panicky feelings were still there, a little. And my heart was going a million miles an hour. But I wasn't dead. So *that* was a bonus. And it was kind of exciting seeing shops and buses and people rushing around. I shrugged. 'Think so.'

We passed the hairdresser, the shoe shop, the optician. Mrs Afolabi waved at us from the greengrocer, and we waved back. We went past school, which made me feel all funny inside, even though it was closed. Eventually, we reached the very edge of Accringham, where the houses ended and the fields began.

I checked my phone. 'It's here.'

We were standing at the end of a muddy, pot-holed track, with a gate in front of us. A dog was yapping its head off in the distance. There was a sign on the gate.

Anna turned to me. 'What's plan B?'

'There is no plan B.' I took her arm. 'Come on. You can't leave me now.'

She stuffed the sleeve of her cardigan in her mouth and nodded.

The gate had a zillion locks, so we clambered over it, lifting Useless, and went down the track, dodging the puddles. The yapping was getting louder and more frantic. The track bent round to the right, to another gate, hanging off its hinges at an angle. Through the gate was a decrepit shed with a corrugated iron roof, where the barking was coming from. Beyond that was a huge muddy field, with a few old caravans dotted around.

A bell dinged and Archie came skidding around the corner on his bike. He braked right in front of us, spraying us with mud. 'I told you it was a dump.'

I wiped my face. 'I wouldn't call it a dump.'

'I would,' muttered Anna.

We followed him through the gate. As soon as he went into the shed, the barking stopped. He came out carrying a tiny, fluffy white dog. 'Meet Jaws.'

I blinked. '*That's* what was making all the noise?'

A bald man with a potato-shaped head, wearing filthy overalls, emerged from the shed.

'Here's Dad,' said Archie.

Archie's dad nodded at us. 'I think I might have just what you're looking for.' He led us to the far corner of the field and pointed at a massive old beast of a caravan, surrounded by nettles. It must have once been white, but now it was more of a grey-green sludgey colour. The roof was darker, covered in slime.

'It's not pretty and it'll need cleaning up, but look . . .' He gestured for us to follow him around the side of the caravan, and lifted a panel to reveal a hatch. 'The previous owner converted it to sell Japanese street food, but it never took off. Not much call for sushi in Accringham.'

'So you could sleep in it *and* sell pizzas,' said Archie.

Anna nudged me. 'You wouldn't be scared,' she whispered, 'because your home would always be with you.'

'Come inside, I'll give you a tour. Hold your nose.' Archie's dad opened the door, and we carefully made our way through the nettles and climbed up into the caravan. Useless immediately jumped up onto one of the bench seats running down each side.

The first thing that hit me was the smell. Like a wet towel had been left to rot. There were windows, but they were green, so they didn't let in much light. But even through the gloom, I could see how roomy it was. I could imagine how it would look if it was cleaned up and given a bit of attention.

'It's much bigger than it looks from the outside,' said Anna.

'Like the TARDIS,' I muttered, more to myself than anyone else, but Archie's dad twisted around to look at me.

'Another *Doctor Who* fan?' he said.

'You like *Doctor Who*?' I asked.

'Not me.' He pointed at Archie. 'Him.'

Archie scowled. 'No, I don't.'

'Yes, you do,' said his dad. 'You've even got *Doctor Who* pyj—'

'Da-ad,' said Archie, through gritted teeth.

The front half of the caravan was set up as a tiny kitchen. The smell in there was even worse.

'Damp,' said Archie's dad, pointing to a patch of green mould in the corner.

There was a counter with an oven above it and a fridge underneath. Opposite was another counter and the service hatch. Archie's dad led us back through the main section of the caravan, pointing out a fold-away table next to one of the benches. At the back of the caravan was a sliding door hiding a loo with a shower head above it.

I peered into the loo. Something dark and slimy was lurking in it.

Anna looked over my shoulder. 'A frog!'

'That's good luck, isn't it? A frog in the bog?' laughed Archie's dad.

Archie caught my eye and puffed out his cheeks as we went back into the middle of the caravan, as if to say *He's mad*.

'Where's the bedroom?' asked Anna.

Archie's dad laughed, revealing surprisingly white teeth. 'You're standing in it.' He took the stained cushion off the bench that Useless wasn't lying on. Then he lifted something and folded something else, and as if by magic, it turned into a bed. He pointed at the other bench. 'That one does the same.' He looked at me. 'So . . . what do you think? You'd be doing me a favour, to be honest. No one wants a caravan with a hole in the side, and it's taking up space.'

I peered through the grimy window at the empty field. There was *masses* of space. 'It's really kind of you, but . . . um . . .' *How could I tell him we couldn't afford it? There's no way the money we'd made from the magical pizzas would stretch to a caravan!*

He squeezed my shoulder. 'Think of it as a loan. You can borrow it for as long as you like. Archie said he owes you, big time.'

I looked at Archie. My stomach felt all bubbly, like I'd just necked one of those really big bottles of Coke. 'Really?'

Archie grinned at me. 'Really.'

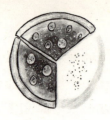

Chapter Eighteen

BEEP! BEEP!

Archie's dad beeped the horn as we pulled up opposite the shop. We were sitting in the front of his truck, towing the caravan behind us.

Dad ran out of the shop as we piled onto the pavement. 'You haven't been outside for weeks then you disappear off the face of the—'

'Afternoon.' Archie's dad crossed the road, wiped an oily hand on his overalls and clapped Dad on the shoulder. 'Can I leave it there?'

Dad frowned at the greasy mark on his shirt. 'Leave what where?'

I grabbed his arm. 'The caravan. Archie's dad said we could borrow it!' I dragged him over the road. 'Welcome to our new home!'

He stared at it. His eyes were so wide, I worried his

eyeballs might fall out. 'Our new *home*?'

'It doesn't look much from the outside, but the inside's amazing. Well . . . it will be. Hold on.' I ran around the back of the caravan and hopped on board, then opened the hatch and leant out. 'Look! We can drive around the country selling pizzas. We'll go on adventures, like you and Mum. Come and see!'

A couple of seconds later, Dad stepped into the caravan, followed by Anna and Useless. I pulled Dad to the front. 'Here's the kitchen. It's got a normal oven but we can swap it for a pizza oven . . . you know, one of those little ones.' We squeezed past Anna, and I opened the sliding door at the back of the caravan. 'Check it out! You can have a shower and go to the loo at the same time.'

Dad scratched his chin. 'O-kay.'

I closed the door and sat on one of the benches. 'And this is the bedroom.'

He went a bit pale. '*This* is the bedroom?'

'The benches fold down to make beds. And we can put this table up for mealtimes.'

Anna looked from me to Dad and back again. 'He hates it.'

I stood up, biting my lip. 'It was just an idea. We can give it back.' I glimpsed Archie's dad through the hatch, rolling his eyes.

Dad opened the oven, then poked his head into the fridge. A huge smile crept over his face as he turned to me. 'I *love* it!' He swept me up in a tight squeeze. It was lucky he was holding me up, because my legs went all shaky. In that moment, with Dad's arms around me, I knew that all my worries were for nothing. It was suddenly so obvious – it wasn't *where* you lived, it was *who* you lived with that was important.

I stood back to get my breath. 'I think Mum would have liked it.'

There was a short silence. Dad's eyes were shining like stars. 'She'd have *loved* it.' He put an arm around my shoulders and gave me another hug, then pulled back and studied my face. 'So . . . how was it? Going outside?'

I blinked. In all the excitement, I'd forgotten about that. 'It was OK.'

Dad beamed at me. 'I'm so proud of you.' He kissed the top of my head. 'Let's look at this kitchen. I might even be able to find a second-hand pizza oven that'll fit.'

'Really?'

'Sure!' he said, his voice rising in excitement as he went into the kitchen. 'We can put shelves up here for the pizza boxes and the toppings.' Poking his head out of the hatch, he slapped the outside of the caravan. 'The menu can go here.' He came back into the bedroom and sat down on one of the benches. Useless leapt up and flopped down with her head on Dad's lap, just as the end of a spring boinged out of the cushion. Dad laughed. 'Which side do you want?'

'I'll go here.' I sat on the bench opposite him.

Anna was opening and closing cupboards. 'How're you going to fit your Lego and computer and everything in here?'

'I don't think I'll have time for any of that stuff.' I glanced at Dad. 'We'll be too busy selling pizzas and exploring, won't we?'

He leant forwards. 'Let's go to Scotland. I can show you where Mum was brought up.'

'Yes!' I felt my cheeks reddening with excitement.

'Can we go to Loch Ness? We could sell our first pizza to the Loch Ness Monster? And Cornwall – I've always wanted to go to Cornwall.'

Dad laughed. 'We've only got a few weeks left of the summer holidays, so we'll see what we can do.' He paused. 'That is, if you're planning on going back to school next term.'

I glanced at Anna. 'I think I will.'

'Yes!' She pushed her glasses up. 'Can I come with you? On your trip?'

'I think we'll start on our own,' said Dad, 'but if we're driving past Accringham you could join us for a few days?'

'And Useless?' she asked.

Dad's eyes twinkled as he stroked Useless's ears. 'I'm sure we could squeeze her in.'

Anna looked at me. 'Promise you'll come and get us?'

'Promise,' I said. My heart felt like it was about to explode with joy. This was going to be the best home ever.

★

Dad and I took the caravan back to Archie's dad's place, and we spent the next few days polishing it and spraying it with silver metallic paint until it gleamed. Archie and his dad helped as well, power-washing inside and out, fixing the plumbing and the electrics. Anna painted a sign over the hatch, which read 'Pete's Pizza Van', and we hung spotty bunting below that. Dad made little window boxes, whistling all the while, and we filled them with brightly coloured flowers in pots.

Inside, we made it all homely, with my *Doctor Who* duvet and my camel wall-hanging, and we stuck up our family photos. We scrubbed the tiny kitchen and Dad persuaded his friend to give us a great deal on a second-hand pizza oven. We didn't put up the old fridge magnets – Dad said we could buy new ones wherever we went – or the reward chart, which I gleefully ripped up.

The afternoon before we were due to head off, I asked Dad if I could have one last look around the pizza shop, on my own. We still had a spare key, and no one else had moved in, so Dad kept watch while I unlocked the door and stepped into my old home.

The oven hadn't been lit for a few days, and even though it was warm outside, I felt shivery. I stood in the middle of the shop and looked around. Craig had helped us move the bath and clear up the rubble, and we'd spent ages wiping away the dust, but there was still a huge hole in the ceiling. I wandered into the kitchen, then went upstairs. The wall on the stairs had little rectangular shapes on it, where the photos had been taken down.

'Mum?' My voice echoed around my bedroom, although it didn't feel like my bedroom anymore, with none of my stuff in it. 'Mum?' I repeated, looking up. 'You're coming with us, right?'

There was no answer, but I felt a warm glow in my chest.

I smiled. Mum wasn't in the pizza shop, just like she wasn't in the caravan. She was right here, in my heart. I couldn't possibly forget about her. She'd be with me, wherever I went.

That evening, Anna and I sat outside the caravan. It was seven o'clock and still warm. We were parked in Craig's pub car park – there was a grassy area at the back with a table and chairs, and Dad had strung up some lights between the trees and the caravan. Anna was strumming her guitar, Useless was wriggling around on the grass with her legs in the air, and Dad was in the pub, having a last pint with Craig. The briefcase was on the table between us.

I picked up my phone. 'Professor Silva Tregoning.' I typed her name into Google. 'It's time to track you down and reunite you with your potions.'

The first few posts were about her being sacked from Firdale Pharmaceutical. In all of them she was described as a maverick – a rule-breaker – just like the newspaper article we'd found in the briefcase.

I peered at the screen. 'Remember Sanjay Citra, the guy who sacked her? It says he picked her for the job because she was "ethical, reliable and responsible". That doesn't sound like a maverick.'

Anna put down her guitar. 'Where is she now?'

I scrolled back up to the top of the first page, and looked at the date of the last post. 'That's odd. There's no mention of her at all after March 2008, when she was sacked. It's like she disappeared off the face of the earth.'

Anna's eyes narrowed. '*Very* odd. The whole thing sounds a bit fishy—'

'Pete?' Archie walked around the back of the caravan. 'I forgot to give this back.' He passed me a brown bottle – the Shrink potion.

'Thanks, Archie.' He stood with his hands in his pockets, a little awkwardly, while I put the potion in the briefcase with the others.

'What are you going to do with them?' asked Anna.

I shrugged. 'I guess we'll have to take them with us. I'll lock them in a cupboard.'

Archie frowned. 'Why? Aren't you making magical pizzas anymore?'

'Nope. Back to normal pizzas. Dad says we'll find fresh new toppings wherever we go. Seafood by the

coast, haggis in Scotland, Wensleydale cheese in . . .
um . . .'

'Wensleydale?' he said.

'Exactly.'

He tugged on his ear. 'Before you go, I just wanted
to say . . . you know . . . about me being such a . . .'

'Are you trying to apologise for being a total loser?'
said Anna. I kicked her under the table.

He cleared his throat. 'I guess I was a bit . . . you
know . . . jealous.'

I frowned. 'Jealous? Of me?'

He lowered his voice. 'You didn't even go to school
and you still got top marks for everything last term.'

'I . . . er . . .'

'While mine went through the floor, 'cos you
weren't around for me to copy.'

'Oh . . . sorry about that,' I said. 'You must be a *bit*
clever though.'

'What?' said Archie.

'Your spirit animal's a pig,' I said. 'And pigs are
famously really clever.'

He snorted. I don't think he meant to sound like
a pig, but he did. I caught Anna's eye and we both

laughed, then Archie joined in and snorted again, which made us laugh even harder.

His phone beeped. 'That's Dad. I'd better go.' He slapped the caravan with his hand. 'Don't drive too fast. Dad's caravans have a habit of falling apart.' He waved as he walked off. 'Have fun.'

'Bye, Archie,' I said.

'Bye, Archie.' Anna picked up her guitar. 'Did you really mean that about not doing magical pizzas?'

I nodded. 'I'm done with magic.' I grinned at her. 'For now.'

THE END

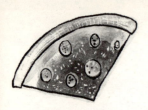

Easy Pizza Margherita Recipe
(serves 2-4)

Ingredients

300 g strong bread flour

1 tsp instant yeast

1 tsp salt

1 tbsp olive oil

100 ml passata (or canned tomatoes)

Handful fresh or dried basil

125 g mozzarella

Handful cherry tomatoes, halved

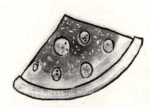

Method

1. The base: tip the flour into a bowl, then stir in the yeast and salt. Make a well, pour in 200 ml warm water and the olive oil. Stir with a wooden spoon until you have a soft, fairly wet dough. Turn onto a lightly floured surface and knead for 5 mins until smooth. Cover with a tea towel and set aside for an hour or two, to rise.

2. The sauce: mix the passata and basil, then add a pinch of salt.

3. Roll out the dough: give it a quick knead, then split into two balls. On a floured surface, roll out the dough into two very thin rounds. Lift them onto two floured baking sheets.

4. Top and bake: heat the oven to 240C/220C fan/ gas 8. Smooth sauce over bases with back of spoon. Scatter with mozzarella and tomatoes. Bake for 8-10 mins until crisp.

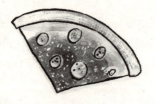

Acknowledgments:

To make a truly great pizza requires expert hands. A book is the same, so I'm hugely grateful to everyone who helped bring Pizza Pete to life.

The BIGGEST thanks go to Bella Pearson. This book would not be here if you hadn't plucked my story out of a Guppy Open Submission competition. I'll be forever grateful to you for seeing potential in me.

I couldn't believe my luck when my first choice of illustrator came on board - the incredible Sarah Horne. Thank you, Sarah, for bringing Pete's shenanigans to life.

Huge thanks to Catherine Alport and Liz Scott for PR prowess, Ness Wood and Alison Gadsby for dazzling design, Adamma Okonkwo for careful copyediting, Hannah Featherstone for punctilious proofreading, Colyn Allsopp for tricky typesetting and everyone at Michael O'Mara books for skilful sales.

I am eternally grateful to Steve Blackman and James Pratt for beta reading, and Will Dobson for his eagle-eyed attention to detail. They share the gratitude pizza with the rest of the Dead Pets Society: Vendela Ahlstrom, Georgina Frame, Piu das Gupta, Jayne Leadbetter, Emma Lyndon-Stanford, Lucy Mohan, Philippa Peall, Krysia Pepper, Becks Perkin and Rebecca Wood. You know I wouldn't be here without you.

Jez McGivern – thanks for kicking me over the start line. I blame you entirely for my messy house and neglected children.

A hearty thank you to all my supportive friends – you know who you are. I love you all.

I grew up in a house full of books, and I want to thank my wonderful parents for instilling a love of reading in me. Mum – thanks for taking me to Wimbledon library every week after school. Allie - it all started with the AJM magazine (even though I was only allowed to do the colouring in). Jamie – you saved my life when my duvet caught fire while I was reading under the covers. I wish you and Dad were here to share this moment. Kerri – thanks for all your advice.

To my darling Immie, Freddie and Tallulah. Thank you for reading endless versions of this book, and for keeping quiet (sort of) when I'm writing. The upside of having a slightly absent mother is you've finally learnt the location of the dishwasher.

None of this would have been possible without my husband. Thank you, Jim, for your brilliant plot ideas, your unwavering support and for always believing in me.

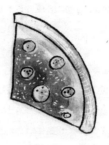

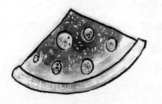

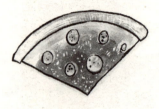

Carrie Sellon

Carrie Sellon was born in Bristol and now lives in Hampshire with her husband, three children, dog friend (Mabel), tortoise friend (Sid), chicken friends (Bluebell and Snowy) and thirty thousand bee friends (Andy, Pamela, Ellie, Mark . . . you get the idea).

She used to travel the world making wildlife films for the BBC, but now, much like Pizza Pete, prefers hanging out at home, eating too much pizza.

Pizza Pete and the Perilous Potions is her first book.

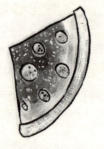

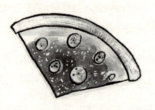

GUPPY
BOOKS

Guppy Books is an independent children's publisher based in Oxford in the UK, publishing exceptional fiction for children of all ages.

Small and responsive, inclusive and communicative, Guppy Books was set up in 2019 and publishes only the very best authors and illustrators from around the world.

From brilliantly funny illustrated tales for five-year-olds and page-turning magical adventures for ten-year-olds, to inspiring and thought-provoking novels for young adults, Guppy Books promises to publish something for everyone. If you'd like to know more about our authors and books, visit the Guppy Aquarium on YouTube.

We hope that our books bring pleasure to young people of all ages, and also to the grown-ups sharing these books with them.

Bella Pearson
Publisher

www.guppybooks.co.uk

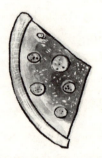